Winds of Change

(and a whisper)

stories by
Edward P.G. Field

One Printers Way
Altona, MB R0G 0B0
Canada

www.friesenpress.com

First Edition — 2021

Cover illustration by Andrew Chandler

ISBN
978-1-03-912625-1 (Hardcover)
978-1-03-912624-4 (Paperback)
978-1-03-912626-8 (eBook)

1. FICTION, SATIRE

Distributed to the trade by The Ingram Book Company

Comments from readers:

Full Circle: "A cautionary tale! So well written." —**Luella Meighen**

"Between an allegory and parable . . . a moving commentary on society." —**Mark Robinson**

The Alphabet Coalition: "We immensely enjoyed the story . . . priceless. Keep the stories coming!" —**Bert and Wieke Moes**

The Sound of One Hand: "Tongue in cheek! So true of our society today" **Ingrid Roseweir**

"Hilarious, witty and playful." —**Margaret Cameron**

"Another brilliant story that masterfully topped up our daily quota of laughter." —**Mark Robinson**

Paintings and Crabs: "A most enjoyable, thought provoking and insightful read. The image of the crab's growth is one that will stay with me." —**Rev. Canon Mike Stewart**

"Wonderfully tender and insightful." —**John Ainsworth**

Divining: "I think it's both subtle and clever to introduce so unexpectedly a picture of grace in operation!" —**June Lepsoe**

Paciencia: "I shared the narrative with a number of seasoned storytellers. Piet Torenvliet, Inge de Visser and I myself give Edward's creativity a thumbs up." —**Apko Nap** *(author of the storytelling course manual, "Ears acquire eyes when you listen")*

"I am waiting for the publication of your Stories from the Field which I hope will someday appear and I can have a lovely volume of these heartwarming tales to hold in my hands and curl up with in a nice armchair." —**Jan Vanderhill**

With thanks to the many friends
who have read my stories and provided feedback
and
with special thanks to Patricia
who has patiently listened to these tales numerous times,
offering helpful suggestions and encouragement

"The Lord said, "Go out and stand on the mountain in the presence of the Lord, for the Lord is about to pass by." Then a great and powerful wind tore the mountains apart and shattered the rocks before the Lord, but the Lord was not in the wind. After the wind there was an earthquake, but the Lord was not in the earthquake. After the earthquake, came a fire, but the Lord was not in the fire. And after the fire came a gentle whisper. When Elijah heard it, he pulled his cloak over his face . . ."(1 Kings 19:11-13 NIV)

Foreword

The following collection begins with a few tales, some satirical, responding to winds of change blowing currently through North America. G.K. Chesterton observed that "Satire . . . presupposes a standard . . . . The curious disappearance of satire from our literature is an instance of the fierce things fading for want of any principle to be fierce about." Satire is not always amusing; but whether we laugh or wince, hopefully there is fresh perspective.

Jesus, the Master Storyteller, opened our understanding with parables which we still marvel at. To dismiss "The Good Samaritan" because it is fiction would be foolish. We recognize the types of people included in the story—and perhaps we see ourselves. Truth can be subtly contained in stories which are revealing as well as entertaining. May you find some of that here!

So many of the gems of life we stumble across ***en famille***. A few stories, then, have to do with the generations of one family, the Payntons.

Just as the hubris of each year is thankfully muted for the holy days of Christmas, there are four Christmas stories for the hearth.

Finally, there is a story of a small community which has survived nuclear war. Many in the village become convinced they must set out on a journey. The story is about what urges some people to consider leaving what they have always known, the opposition which they encounter from others, and what may be discovered during the journey—and at its end.

"After the wind . . . came a gentle whisper." (1 Kings 19:11-13)

Throughout this collection of tales, I hope you can detect a gentle whisper.

Edward Field

Table of Contents

Winds of change **1**

Full Circle 3

The Alphabet Coalition 13

Bamboo Princess 19

Barbara and the Sword of Damocles 23

The Zoo and the Ark 28

The Sound of One Hand 34

Reassessment 39

All in the family **53**

Force of Habit 54

Essentials 59

Paintings and Crabs 63

Uncle Sid's Legacy 70

Paciencia! 80

Academic 87

Golden Boy 94

Divining 98

Christmas at last **107**

'Tis the Season 108

Mosslawns.com 112

"Who knit ya?" 118

All God's Creatures 128

Beyond **135**

The Bridge 136

Winds of change

Full Circle

Manchmal, British Columbia, is a horsey community. Rolling grasslands and trails around crystalline lakes lend themselves to the horse ranches and hobby farms. The real economy is in open-pit mining and a small pulp and paper mill, but anyone who lives in Manchmal lives and breathes horses. Kids grow up in the 4-H Club which is dominated by horse-talk. There's a July rodeo that attracts big names from Alberta and Montana, and Manchmal is fiercely proud that its own champions place well in most of the competitions.

On the south end of Manchmal, down by the mud flats is the Worster family homestead on a farm named "Full Circle", a reference to a ring of low hills seen from the house. Harry Worster doesn't work the farm the way his dad did, but he's reluctant to sell the old place, so he rents out the fields and keeps a small parcel for a hobby farm which he and Jillian run. Much of the week Harry is out at the mill, and Jillian is left to milk a couple of cows, and give riding lessons to neighborhood kids.

Fifteen years back, little Denny Worster loved horses so much he acted like one. It was cute when Denny, aged 4, galloped around a paddock and copied the ponies' neighing as best he could. Grampa Worster laughed so hard he wet himself! That Christmas the grandparents gave Denny his first saddle—as it turned out, the beginning of great things. Bursting with excitement, and leaving other presents unwrapped, the child eagerly dragged his saddle to the stable to try it out. Scarcely a month later, neighbours were remarking on his natural talent for riding.

Everything for Denny's fifth birthday had a horse motif. The invited kids dressed as cowboys and went through a maze of games set up in the paddock. There was a contest lassoing stumps, then they laughed at each other being blindfolded and trying to pin the tail on a donkey poster. There was huge laughter when one blindfolded child missed the donkey altogether and pinned the tail on the farmer in the poster. Because Denny begged incessantly, Grandpa blindfolded him again so that Denny could show off how fast he could put together the pieces of a bridle just by the feel. The party finished with a giant horse piñata.

By age 6 Denny was really confident on the ponies. One day he pleaded with his mother Jillian to let him try the pole bending routine after the older kids had finished their lesson—and who'd have believed he was just about as fast as 10 year-old Walt Schmidt! By age 7 he was in the Juniors for the rodeo, an amazing barrel-racer!

That was the summer after grade 2. It was difficult for Denny in September when school started up again. Each day before riding his bike to Sandpines Elementary, Denny would be in the stable talking softly to the ponies and making sure they got their morning feed of sweet-smelling meadow hay. Even at school, for the 20 minutes of Sustained Silent Reading, he invariably had his head in a library book on horse breeds, horse history or famous cowboys. At recess times and lunch, Denny amused his classmates by galloping around the climbing bars, charging at the girls on the swings and snorting. Fun for everyone until one day he got carried away, rolled his lips back and nipped one of the girls on her thigh. The two-day suspension was more of a reward than a punishment, as he got to spend the whole time helping his mum with stable chores. Kids avoided him after that, except for the group science projects where they had no choice, and Denny became a loner. Nipping other students happened on and off, with time spent at home, until grade 8, when Doug Bartell threatened to beat the crap out of Denny if he ever did it again. So Denny became sullen and even more reclusive, rarely speaking unless asked a question by a teacher, and leaving school as soon as the bell rang.

But he talked with horses and, incredibly, they seemed to talk back! Throwing his school pack down by the kitchen table, Denny would head straight for the stable where he approached the ponies with a low, soft, greeting nicker. Immediately the heads would come up, faces relaxed, and one after another would repeat the nicker back to him. It was uncanny! Harry and Jillian Worster wondered whether their son might go on to be a breeder or a trainer. Being a veterinarian seemed out of the question with his abysmal science marks.

The summer after Grade 9 something radical changed in Denny. He would not saddle up to go on trail rides and shook his head fretfully when his mother talked to him about the July rodeo. To his parents' dismay, Denny ceased talking altogether, instead responding to all questions by neighing, snorting, sneezing, squealing, grunting and groaning. The rodeo came and went without Denny riding in any competitions—not even in the flag race, which he had won for years. In September there was no point in trying to send him to school; he wouldn't go. Neighbours could overhear nightly arguments, raised voices in the Worster farmhouse as Jillian and Harry thrashed out their options for how to deal with the growing problem. Gradually it became common knowledge that Denny was no longer living in his house, but in the stable, where he bedded down on wood shavings beside the horses. He had discarded his clothes and walked around naked, crouched over, his hands on the ground—a source of huge amusement to former classmates, who came as close as the distant pasture rails would allow spectators. Jillian, greatly embarrassed, but at a loss about what to do, brought him meals at the regular times. Some of these he slurped up from the plate left on the stable floor. He drank water from the horse buckets, nibbled at the alfalfa bales or oats, and even licked the salt block. His father Harry knew he couldn't expect Jillian to deal with the change of events all by herself. Reluctantly, he cleaned out the stable 4 times a day and scrubbed the water bucket daily rather than once a week.

Apart from two Shetland ponies, the Worster family had 3 larger horses used for riding lessons, trail riding and barrel racing. There was Dusty, the chestnut Morgan, 5 feet to the withers, and two quarter horses, a sorrel mare and a bay stallion. The bay was 15 hands high and 1100 pounds—not dangerous to Denny had he been standing upright, but a threat to the boy as he walked around on all fours. Out of compassion, Harry arranged to buy a Falabella horse, 30 inches to the withers, which could be paired with Denny for pulling a cart.

Time has a strange way of making us accept what we cannot change. A full year passed. It seemed terrible at first, but nights of Jillian crying herself to sleep had to give way to some kind of acceptance. When Denny pointed to the tails of the horses and to his own bare backside, she realized it was a plea for a tail of his own. And her mother's heart full of distress led her to discuss the issue with her friend, a young veterinarian surgeon. Over a coffee in the farmhouse kitchen, Jillian confided in young Dr. Krantz, wondering aloud whether he might be able to fit a pony tail for Denny. At first he laughed, then fell silent when he realized how in earnest she was. Dead serious, she asked, "Would it be any more controversial than docking a dog's tail or declawing a cat or cosmetic surgery for humans—you know, like a face-lift or a breast implant?" The more Krantz thought about this, the more doable it sounded. Within only a few weeks a suitable tail was found following an accident at a farm in the next valley. Denny was given a general anesthetic and the tail was surgically attached. Denny was obviously sore, but just as obviously elated with his tail. He sidled up to Misty, a Shetland mini, to compare her tail with his.

News of Denny's operation was the talk of Manchmal for a few days, then it became stale, as all news does. There was another brief flurry of upset over Denny being placed together with the Worster Shetlands for animal therapy. In early July some Manchmal citizens wrote angrily to the newspaper when they discovered that Denny the Pony would be in the July parade, but parade officials had been persuaded by Dr. Krantz and Mrs. Worster to consider whether Denny had not virtually become a pony. Several editorials came out arguing in favour of Denny the Pony--who could deny that he trotted and cantered like a horse, or that he lived like a horse, in short, that he was happy that way?—until objection was seen as the mark of a red-neck. That was how Denny made his debut in the same July parade where he had, in former years, ridden as Denny the Rodeo Kid.

Five year old Megan Ford, whose family had just moved to Manchmal that week, came with her parents to watch the parade. When she saw Denny down on all fours, wearing a saddle and being led by a halter along with the two Shetland minis and the Falabella—when she saw this, she couldn't believe her eyes. She burst out laughing, pointing at Denny and screaming, "Look at the boy with the horses!" Her mother, sensing a bristling from people in the crowd, quickly whisked Megan into a nearby store, but the damage was done; Denny was weeping and neighing desperately to prove his identity. That night Megan's parents were informed of the seriousness of the incident. It was made clear to them what the town's folk had all come to believe, that people are what they think they are, and it is cruel to tell them otherwise. The little girl herself remained confused but her parents privately assured her that she had done nothing wrong; someone had just wanted them to move to a different place. In a sense that was true.

The Fords had not been part of the town's evolving views. They tried, nonetheless, to settle into Manchmal society. Dr. Ford was welcomed into a family practice by an overworked GP, and enthusiastically added to the on-call list for the Regional Hospital. Little Megan was enrolled in Sandpines Elementary and her mother Anita volunteered as a classroom aide. Then the unpleasantness of the parade incident faded with the excitement of Megan's first year in school. Ms. Vanderbilt turned out to be a wonderfully innovative Kindergarten teacher, teaching the alphabet with clay, using marshmallows for math, bringing in grandparents to tell stories, taking the children for frequent nature walks, weekly reconfiguring an obstacle course out of donated tires—her repertoire of ideas was impressive! She had recently developed a unit on animals and had each child choose an animal, find out all about it, then do a short presentation to the class. Megan chose to tell about raccoons, and her mother made her a raccoon costume to help with her presentation. At the end of each presentation, Ms. V. asked the child to tell what would be fun about being the animal. There was lots of laughter. Then there was an announcement of a planned Kindergarten field trip to visit Denny the Pony.

So the issue wouldn't go away after all. The Fords felt quite unhappy with this development and planned to keep Megan home on the day of the field trip. As it happened, on the week of the planned field trip, Dr. Krantz phoned the school to explain Denny had become quite sick and would not be able to receive his little visitors. Parents and other townspeople who expressed concern were told Denny had a problem digesting groats. This was partly true, but it was much more serious than that. Because of the way he lay in the stable, no one had noticed the gangrenous tissue around Denny's grafted tail. Dr. Krantz treated him daily without moving him from the farm, but what the vet had feared did eventually happen: Denny died.

Jillian and Harry Worster were devastated, reproaching themselves for not having more carefully monitored the area of tail surgery. They spoke to few people about the loss of their son, but the news leaked out and oozed into every conversation until it was impossible to think of a quiet burial for Denny. The mayor declared that this was a loss to the whole community and that a service of memorial would allow people to share how much Denny had touched their lives. Reluctantly, the Worsters agreed.

The service was attended by virtually the whole town. Various citizens spoke about Denny. These included his mother, of course, and Dr. Krantz. Mayor Shelby promised a Denny monument would be created for the park. The principal of Sandpines Elementary praised Ms. Vanderbilt for her encouragement of all children to think outside the box as Denny had, to realize their dreams, to embrace whatever identity truly appealed to them.

"Really?" muttered Trevor Ford to his wife. "What about biological reality?" To his chagrin, he had been overheard by Ms. V. herself, who rebuked him sternly from behind.

"Reality is what we make it, Dr. Ford. Our culture is changing and we must be open to change."

Their stay in the town had only lasted a few months when the Fords sold their recently acquired home and moved to Cottonwood, just an hour away. For Dr. Ford, work at the Regional Hospital might stay the same, but their new address meant Megan could enrol for Grade One in Cottonwood Elementary. When Trevor and Anita met parents and teachers at the new school, they were barraged with questions about the situation in Manchmal. "Wasn't there a way that Worster boy could have been helped?" "Couldn't his death have been prevented?" "How could everyone just have accepted his behaviour?"

"Look," protested Trevor Ford to a group of incredulous Cottonwood citizens, "Our family is new to this area. But from what I understand, somebody thought it was the kindest way to treat the young man, and other people felt awkward about disagreeing. Bit by bit the whole community went along with it, just kind of let it happen. Then it became a cause. Now, if you want to live in Manchmal, you have to believe that a child can actually become a horse, or you keep your mouth shut. It's gone from being kind to Denny to encouraging others to become just like him."

Ford told them about Mayor Shelby, the dedication of the Denny Monument, and the new program of Sandpines Elementary, a primary grades discovery program titled "Which animal lives in you?" By the end of his account, his audience couldn't keep quiet. One Cottonwood man blurted out in exasperation.

"So they've made a hero out of the kid! They're actually going to screw up the lives of other children? What kind of teacher would come up with an asinine school program like that? Honestly, who thinks up this stuff, and what kind of school board would approve it?!"

Trevor smiled a little at the comment. He pulled a folded newspaper from under his arm and opened it to show his new neighbours. There, on the front page of the Manchmal Herald, was Ms. Vanderbilt holding up a copy of the new program; School Board members stood beaming on either side of her.

Little Megan knew only the excitement of a larger bedroom in the new house and new friends, some right next door. She adored her grade one teacher. Parents of school children naturally got to know each other's families as they waited for their kids at the end of the day, or helped with classroom activities. Anita formed some close friendships.

Trevor Ford opened a new medical practice in Cottonwood, but continued his involvement on Mondays and Tuesdays at the Regional Hospital. Through conversations with hospital colleagues, he learned of changes within the community of Manchmal. There were rumblings of discontent within Sandpines School. Several families had withdrawn their children and were homeschooling. By the end of Megan's grade two year, news filtered through to Cottonwood that Manchmal's school district had not only discontinued the animal discovery program, but fired its author, Ms. Vanderbilt. The Fords listened to a radio talk show in which various Manchmal people were interviewed. These included the principal of Sandpines Elementary, who claimed that no one had ever really believed in the program except for its author. Ms. V. countered that she had only created the program at the request of the School Board. Of course she didn't believe in the idea that a child could actually become an animal just by willing it. "How ridiculous!" she said.

The Denny Monument was quietly removed one evening from its place in Memorial Park. Mayor Shelby spoke privately with Dr. Kranz, the vet, who agreed to take the bronze statue out to Full Circle Ranch and offer it to the Worsters. This was no easy job, since the life-size bronze with its base weighed over 600 pounds. Two park maintenance workers unbolted it from the base then lifted the two sections into the back of the vet's pick-up. Harry and Jillian felt awkward when he arrived unannounced with this gift, but thanked him. The three of them struggled to lift the pieces into the bucket of Harry's tractor, then it was unloaded in the barn where Denny had passed away. Harry reassembled it that evening then he and Jillian stood back, looking more closely at the monument which had stood in the park for three years. It depicted Denny naked, on all fours, set on a grassy mound. His tail and long hair seemed to be flowing in the wind. On the base were the words, "Denny the Pony." Harry and Jillian stared at it a long time. Jillian cried. They said little. The monument remained in the barn about a week, then Harry used his tractor to excavate a pit where he buried it.

They'd never asked for a statue in the first place. Jillian had never felt at ease with the public focus on her son's obsession. She hadn't wanted him to be a poster child to promote a school program.

She wanted to remember her boy before his sullen unhappiness, before . . . before he lost the will to be human.

In the barn Jillian hung her favourite picture of their son: twelve year old Denny dressed in his familiar jeans, plaid shirt and worn roper boots. The photo was taken after a trail ride when he was sitting without a saddle on Dusty the Morgan, leaning forward to hug the neck of his horse, a look of bliss on his face.

The Alphabet Coalition

When Axlington Bend acquired an air base, there was general euphoria. The new base included a terminal for civilian traffic, eliminating the need to drive two and a half hours out of state to the nearest airport. Construction, infrastructure, and a new shopping center promised creation of 1500 jobs. The boost to local economy—restaurants, schools, businesses—could not be denied.

Not everyone was happy about the new air base when it was up and running. The Axlington Balloon Company had two giant red and white checkered hot air balloons which had for several years regularly sailed across the landscape with tourists from late May to early October. ABC also sold helium balloons of all shapes and sizes for special events. But now the flight of hot air balloons or release of helium balloons could not legally take place within a 7 mile radius of the new airbase, which significantly conflicted with the business of George Rumstead.

George fumed about this. He relocated the two hot air balloons to South Fernway, just beyond the 7 mile limit—not a bad location, but he did need to be more cautious with prevailing winds not taking tourists back into the flight zone. From his downtown location, he continued to sell and deliver helium balloons to parties and events throughout Greater Axlington—until the day Axlington Motors lost a few dozen giant advertising balloons into the atmosphere and a jet pilot complained to the base. George thought this ridiculous, but the official letter from the CO cited two cases in which helium balloons had caused serious problems for air traffic, and threatened legal action if George would not restrict helium balloon sales to outside the flight zone.

"It's a hollow threat," thought George. "I just sell and deliver the balloons. What people do with them is not my problem." Defiantly, he inflated a dozen large balloons bearing his company's ABC initials, loaded them into his van and drove to just within the 7 mile limit, where he released the balloons into the atmosphere. Hastily he exited the scene, then wondered over the next few days whether there might be repercussions. When no letters arrived and no official showed up at his shop, he breathed a sigh of relief. "It's unfair," he thought, "but I'd better toe the line. I'm just one little business against the whole bloody air force." So there were no repeats of defiance, although he did talk about his grievances at the pub on Friday nights after he'd had a few.

On one of those Friday pub nights, he told his buddies how he had released balloons in protest—balloons which bore the letters ABC—and concluded, "But it's gotta be more than just me standing up." Larry was sympathetic. His own 50s diner had lost out to a Food Court inside the new mall. Gord's Hardware, too, had lost sales to a new Mega Work Bench outlet. Who knows how many small town businesses had suffered indirectly because of the new air field?

Gord had an inspiration. Why not release balloons with the initials from their three businesses—add to ABC the initials GH (Gord's Hardware) and OK (the Omelet Kitchen)? It would be harder for the base to come after three businesses. The idea cheered George immediately.

A few days later at 6:30 in the morning, the three friends released bundles of giant balloons from Avon Park, well inside the 7 mile limit. Every balloon taken from George's delivery van had in bold letters the initials of all three businesses. Before noon an angry phone call came from the office of the Wing Commander. ABC was the obvious culprit, even if GH and OK could not be identified. What on earth did George Rumstead think he was doing jeopardizing air safety? This would be the final warning before legal action.

George conferred with his buddies, then called the Axlington Herald which was always looking for local issues. A reporter came over, interviewed George about the situation and took pictures of him bending down to give a birthday balloon to an awestruck toddler. The story ran on page 3 of Saturday's Herald with the headline, "Air Force threatens balloon shop". The reporter had obtained an interview with a spokesperson for the Base, who stated that Mr. Rumstead had been given fair warning, but had apparently deliberately released more balloons despite the danger to incoming planes. George waited eagerly for phone calls of support but no one called. Monday, when he went for a coffee and butter tart at the neighboring bakery, one of the staff said she had seen the article. But that was the extent of any response until the following Saturday's Herald. The opinion page was full of letters about it, most defending the airport's stand, but a few acknowledging that some businesses had been negatively affected by the new base and perhaps should receive compensation.

This mild concession annoyed and agitated George, who walked about his shop restlessly, wondering what his next steps might be. Surely other merchants would support him if he could just talk to them. He had never thought there was much use for the Chamber of Commerce, but he could see now that was a mistake. He phoned the Chamber, and asked for 5 minutes on the agenda of the monthly meeting.

Days ticked by uneventfully until he attended his first meeting of the Chamber of Commerce for Axlington. He introduced himself, explained his problem with the airport flight zone regulations, and asked them to join him in a protest. There was a short discussion in which member after member praised the base for providing employment to the area, as well as a much-used civilian terminal. Under those circumstances, they said, it would be silly to protest. George left, feeling deflated like one of his balloons.

Then, from a quite unexpected source, came support. He got a call from Friends of the Wild Wing, a group concerned with identifying and preserving bird populations. Gisèle Tremblay met him for coffee and explained that her group was keen to join forces in protesting the air field. As it turned out, a pair of Spotted Skuerlinks had been sighted in the area before construction of the airport, and now had not been seen for years. True—there were still Skuerlinks, but no spotted ones apart from those, fifty miles away in the next state. George had never heard of a Skuerlink, but he could sense the seriousness of losing this species from the region.

When they met again to discuss a group protest against the airport, Gisèle introduced George to a tall, lean young man named Dorian who asked about George's setbacks and listened intently to the history.

"Quite right," Dorian said when George had finished. "There should be no need to relocate your business. What was here originally should never have been tampered with. The airport should not be allowed to run roughshod over nature or our pioneer businesses."

George had never considered ABC to be a 'pioneer business', but perhaps he needed to give this some thought. Dorian described his own work with the Axling Valley Botanical Society, which had documented the disappearance of a type of lichen after construction began on the air field.

In a happy daze, George found himself at his next balloon release surrounded by placard waving young people who shared his common cause. The U.S. Air Force was a bully pushing around common folk: George, Gord, Larry and the environmentalists; it was Goliath and David all over again. Gisèle and Dorian both liked the balloon idea, but this time making sure the whole name of each group was printed on the balloon, while making the initials very large. There were Axlington Balloon Company, Gord's Hardware, the Omelet Kitchen, Friends of the Wild Wing, the Axling Valley Botanical Society—in bold letters: ABC, GH, OK, FWW, AVBS. Some letters of the alphabet were missing, so balloons went up with the first or last names of people in the two new groups. Q, X and Z were hard to connect with anyone, but Gisèle said that names of birds, animals or plants could be used. She thought of an Arctic gull named a Xeme. Larry suggested a quince for Q and zebra for Z. Somebody asked whether a Xeme or a Zebra had been displaced by the airport. But that didn't seem to matter anymore; all the alphabet slots had to be filled.

Dorian summed up. "This Alphabet Coalition—the letters on our balloons—represent all individuals, small businesses, groups, animals, plants—the whole of life from A to Z which has been set aside without consultation when government decides to pour concrete." This statement was reported in a front page article for the Axlington Herald, along with photos of excited children releasing helium balloons. George's store, Gord's Hardware and the Omelet Kitchen experienced a boost in customers.

The crowds of people who came for free balloons proved the clincher. How could the Air Force come against hundreds of normal citizens? How could it risk angering a whole community in suing a store which was providing free balloons to their children? In a meeting between the Alphabet Coalition leaders and airport personnel, Wing Commander Jeffries asked what the group hoped to achieve.

George spoke for the group. "It's too late now to set right what's been done, but it's important to show that common people count.

We want an annual Lift Off of balloons, with the base shut down for a day."

Disbelieving laughter greeted this request, but in the end that's exactly what happened. It had to be a paid holiday, or airport employees would have none of it. Even the Chamber of Commerce came on board when they realized the popularity of an annual holiday. There were muted complaints about deflated balloons strewn across the county. Larry replied that standing up for common people carried a price; you couldn't make an omelet without cracking eggs. As owner of the Omelet Kitchen, he should know. Dorian said triumphantly they should demand a shutdown of the airport once a month. The Herald reporter asked Wing Commander Jefferies about this possibility and Jefferies pointed out that any helium balloon day would mean all flights would have to be put on hold—not just the Air Force, but civilian flights, too. Furthermore, Air Force employees would not be given a paid monthly holiday on such days, whatever other employers might decide for their own businesses.

Axlington Bend seems content with one Lift-Off a year. To open the events of that special day, a larger-than-life mammoth-shaped balloon is filled with helium and floated up in a net 200 feet to where it is moored, looming over the runway. This enormous mascot seems fitting when you think that mammoths, too, must have been displaced by the Air Force. The sounds of planes are stilled and families flock to the carnival atmosphere. Dorian represents the Alphabet Coalition in some opening comments over a loud speaker. He tells the crowd never to forget, "This is how it was before the airport wrecked everything." Well, it's a fun day, so nobody pops the balloon.

Bamboo Princess

Helena Troilus was a knockout. Long wavy dark hair that fell to her waist, olive complexion from her Italian mother, aquiline nose, long eyelashes, the shapely figure of a model and a teasing yet suave flair that attracted young men in all her classes. She was good in academics, yet still managed to be most valuable player on the girls' basketball team. She had a friendly, easy, laughing way about her that won over even the girls who felt jealous.

Helena was startlingly beautiful. When she rounded a corner or entered a room unexpectedly, her sudden proximity melted even the toughest guys. It was humorous to watch, the way they uncharacteristically lost their sureness, stammered for words, and ended up with lame inquiries about her health.

That, actually, is how it began. Mark was smitten like the rest, lost for words, but desperate to strike up a conversation with this vision of loveliness. So he jabbered anything to make her stay and talk with him.

"Hey, princess, we're ordering pizza for lunch—how about joining us? D'you like Pepperoni? Pineapple? Mediterranean? Me, I prefer Mediterranean, but I guess you gotta watch your figure, huh? Yeah—maybe you've had too much already. What's that smile for? I'm right, I bet. You're beginning to put on weight, huh? But seriously, you gonna join us for pizza at noon?" On he babbled, witless, unaware that he had planted the seeds of doubt in Helena's mind—doubt about her figure and her weight.

Helena was convinced she might be getting fat—laughable, if you'd seen her slim figure. She became obsessed with avoiding food. First it was fries, potatoes, bread, chocolate, cookies, pastry. Then it was everything except salad and consommé. Finally, in desperation, she took laxatives. By the end of first semester at U of T, she had become unrecognizable, positively gaunt, anorexic, skeletal! A friend told me that Helena had taken to vomiting anything she ate minutes after her meals, meagre as they were.

Helena and her Korean roommate Annie Park dropped out of university and opened a restaurant called The Bamboo Princess, a tiny 15 by 20 foot place in a mall frequented by students. They stocked it with herbal teas, ginseng, Asian soups, spinach noodles and a variety of spicy rice dishes, most of which Helena would taste and rave about without actually eating. She had become as twiggy as a bamboo, and was no longer the beautiful princess of a year before. Nevertheless, her eyes flashed with enthusiasm about her plans for adding seafood to the menu. There was still a charm about her, and a sweetness about Annie that made their place a regular hangout for students from the nearby residences. Their three tables were always occupied.

Annie herself had a normal appetite and worried somewhat about Helena's abstinence. But she was a follower, and meekly agreed to whatever Helena suggested for their life together or their business venture. And that, oddly, is why Annie didn't object when Helena began counselling some of their regular clients about how to lose weight—how to become a "bamboo princess". It seemed harmless at first, but even Annie felt uncomfortable when she overheard Helena explaining how it was possible to enjoy food without keeping it down. That evening Annie gently questioned whether it was right to counsel others to become bulimic. Helena was adamant about it being all right, and within a week Annie decided that it was time to return to her family in Seoul.

Helena's tiny apartment, up the back stairs from The Bamboo Princess, had an empty bedroom for about a week. Then Tisha, the girl she had been counseling about bulimia, asked about moving in and sharing the rent. In fact, Tisha said, she would love to work with Helena in the restaurant. Together they developed a bulimic clientele—all young women who felt relieved and welcomed in this understanding atmosphere. Helena and Tisha sold natural diuretics and laxatives, meals with onion, eggplant, asparagus and watermelon. A rack on the counter offered books on fasting. Their menu included 'binge and purge' items, easy to swallow and easy to bring up again in the washroom at the back.

"Binge and Barf!" mocked one magazine writer. Helena responded in a CBCN interview, "It's not an eating disorder, but a different way of appreciating food. There are millions of us across this continent, and it's time the food industry recognized that."

One of the young women clients moved to Montreal and began her own Bamboo Princess, then before long someone opened another BP in Halifax. The Bamboo Princess has become a restaurant chain advertised on billboards and on the Internet as "a haven for alternative eating".

In Winnipeg, the Bamboo Princess began another line of alternative food service. A young man with an aversion to eating food through his mouth found that he could take all of his meals in liquid form, snuffing it up through a straw in his nose. "The feeling of food in my mouth has always bothered me," he says. The Winnipeg BP has developed 3 or 4 liquid meals for "snorters". Helena would approve, I think. She used to say, "It's a matter of listening to people and providing what they want."

Helena herself passed away last year, just 28 years old. Tisha continues to run the new business and is kept very busy with customers and inquiries. What began with a thoughtless comment to

Helena Troilus in her high school years has blossomed into a new restaurant concept. Many people come into the Bamboo Princess wanting to try ***the bulimic way***, to see whether it suits them. It's a success story Helena would be proud of.

At least, that's what Tisha said at the funeral. Tisha and others took turns at the mic remembering their friend and Tisha ended by saying that everything is beautiful in its own way, bulimia included. "Just look at our Bamboo Princess Helena," she said.

Annie Park had flown in from Seoul for the service honouring Helena Troilus. She listened to the anecdotes and cried and laughed with the others. When she got to the mic, Annie introduced herself as Helena's friend from way back, from U of T days. She told the crowd how gorgeous Helena had been. "Helena continued to be beautiful—a princess—in the way she cared about others. But she was beautiful ***in spite of*** bulimia, not because of it." The room became nervously silent. "I am so sorry for the sickness that claimed the life of my friend."

When Annie sat down, in the eerie quiet it seemed to her that several in the surrounding tableau were as skeletal and hollow-eyed as Helena had been. It was the freeze of a moment, then Tisha invited everyone to the tables with eggplant and asparagus crackers. In the end, Annie's comments didn't spoil the celebration of Helena's life, and the event even turned out to be a good promo for the restaurant.

And that, Annie told me later, is what bothered her about the day. Celebrating Helena as the Bamboo Princess, celebrating the idea which had made her that way, it was all somehow too much like bamboo; it was . . . hollow.

Barbara and the Sword of Damocles

One month ago, in November, Barbara and Eric Morgan were visited by old friends, a retired couple who shared memories of motorcycling together with the Morgans down the Washington coast to California. Talk naturally covered all the intervening years, particularly the lives of their grown children and even grandchildren.

Henry showed Eric a photo of himself and Donna dressed in leathers and sitting astride their recently acquired second-hand Goldwing. "I'm not giving up biking!" Then Henry caught sight of the Morgans' brand new Porsche SUV and he frowned. "Brand new, Eric?" Eric explained that his wife had just had her 70th birthday and the old Explorer had packed it in.

"I thought for once she could get the car she really wanted—new. You know," he said softly so that their wives wouldn't hear, "there was a cancer scare, and well . . . I'm so glad she's alive. The money didn't seem to matter anymore."

Henry looked thoughtful. "But if you're going to buy new, you should be buying electric with that kind of money. We should all be thinking about how to reduce fossil fuel consumption. You know, Eric, we're spending our children's future, ignoring the crisis. Donna and I are thinking about putting in solar panels. What kind of heating system do you guys have?"

"A heat pump," replied Eric uncomfortably, unsure whether that would meet with his friend's approval.

"Yeah, heat pumps are a little better," nodded Henry," but not as good as solar panels and getting off the grid. I'm surprised that you would take a step back and buy a brand new gas guzzler."

"It doesn't consume a lot of gas," protested Eric. "In fact, the engine shuts off every time you have to wait at a red light, so I guess that reduces pollution." The rest of the evening together was taken up with Henry discussing climate change and how most evangelical Christians were ignorant, burying their heads in the sand. Their own church, said Donna, had 'gone green'. People were really gung ho about the environment.

So Barbara felt guilty. She ordered the recommended books from Amazon and read through articles sent to her by Donna. She admired her friend and her own conviction grew. In their local paper Barbara read about a group of high school students distressed over the drying up of the Kigorsky Wetlands. "They're saying climate change is responsible," she told Eric. Her husband, always a skeptic, muttered something about the pulp mill diverting water, but Barbara paid no attention. From the paper she read aloud that the high school students were keen to sue the federal government for climate inaction. A lawyer for the group had told the Gazette, "There is a right to a stable climate and the Canadian government can provide that."

"How could that be so?" scoffed Eric. "These people say Canada is responsible for 2% of human-caused CO2. So if every CO2 emission in Canada could be eliminated, the world's emissions would be reduced by 2%. Would 2% provide a stable climate? And to achieve the 2% reduction, all oil jobs would have to go!"

Oh, well, thought Barbara, we'd be all right. We don't live in Alberta or Saskatchewan. "But that's the price one has to pay to do one's part," she called to Eric as he headed outside. "You're always saying it's important to do one's part. Think how other countries might look at Canada's willingness to scrap the oil industry and do the same themselves!" But she heard the kitchen door close and knew that Eric was no longer in the conversation. It was Tuesday morning and he was making his weekly delivery of home-baked muffins to the Shelter for Women. Should he even be doing that, she wondered, since it meant using gas and contributing to greenhouse gases. She felt alone in facing the looming apocalypse.

The church Moderator back in Toronto had just recently declared that the overriding moral issue of our day is the Climate Crisis. "Christians must realize that saving the world today means saving the environment. Jesus came to save the world. If he were around today, probably Jesus would be chairing the Intergovernmental Panel on Climate Change—or at least supporting it. A world without fossil fuel is the gospel we should be preaching." So there it was—from the very top.

Last Saturday, at the church breakfast, the speaker had talked about living with the Sword of Damocles suspended above them. "If you haven't panicked yet, you ought to!" he said to his gray-haired audience. "Our generation bears the responsibility for this—anyone living through the last 30 years—it's our fault, and it's up to us to set it right."

Barbara thought about his hour long power point presentation—all about responsible thinking versus illusions, denial, avoidance, lies. At the end, he warned against trusting sources without checking their credentials. It occurred to Barbara to ask her friend about their speaker who, it turned out, was a doctor of psychology. Thinking back on the talk, she realized she couldn't remember hearing much about Climate Science itself. Thank heavens she hadn't told Eric!

Well, the speaker was right about one thing, she decided. Living happily would be impossible now, knowing that catastrophe was imminent. It was like the old Greek myth of a sword hanging over Damocles when he chose to switch places with the king. What good was wealth when death was just a hair away? It seemed silly to be even thinking about Christmas presents for anyone.

Barbara had read that China contributed about 29% to human CO2 emissions. But that did not exempt Canada from reducing its 2%. One writer pointed out that, per capita, Canada was worse than China in its CO2 emissions! So eliminate use of fossil fuels—that was what the article had said—and plant more forests to change CO2 back to oxygen for human consumption. That should help with the Earth's mushrooming population—2.6 billion in 1954 to 8 billion now?!

"And all of them selfishly sucking in oxygen without a thought!" remarked her friend Katya when they met for a coffee and talked about the article. Katya informed her later that was her "Ah ha!" moment, her epiphany. That was when she realized her mission, her calling. She knew instinctively how she could be part of the solution.

For months she had run a Yoga class on Monday and Saturday mornings in the church basement. She called it "Jesus and Yoga", popular especially with retirees. The minister herself attended, and applauded Katya's ecumenical embrace of eastern wisdom. So Katya excitedly ran her new idea by Reverend Margo and was enthusiastically affirmed. The Yoga class would now be moved to the main service time on Sunday mornings, and re-titled "The breath of life". Katya would teach the church to slow their hearts, then hold their breath for one full minute. Katya looked triumphantly at her friend. Barbara seemed confused, so Katya explained what should have been obvious.

"When we hold our breath, there is one minute when we do not participate in emitting CO2. For one full minute we save oxygen for the world! You know," she added, "Reverend Margo has been searching for a way to make our Christmas service relevant to the people who come once a year. So we'll begin with a couple of carols everybody knows, like "Jingle Bells", then after "the Breath of Life" time, she wants everyone to circulate to information tables around the church—a table for signing a petition against pipelines, another table with a petition against tanker traffic. Maybe a table where people could meet the MP. We could even have a door prize, like a book on Yoga."

When Barbara told Eric later about Katya's brainwave and "The breath of Life" which they would be doing on Sunday mornings starting with the Christmas service, he smiled.

"Sweetheart," he said slowly, "maybe we need to take a break from church for a while. How about…flying to visit the kids in Mississauga? I think they're all in the Christmas Pageant this year. Their church always has the pageant."

Barbara looked aghast. "Eric! What about the damage done by jet fuel?"

"We haven't seen our grandchildren since last summer," he said gently. "And I think some things are more important than worrying about climate change."

Barbara didn't disagree. Actually, she felt relieved. She found she was breathing more easily.

The Zoo and the Ark

As a teen, Chuck Tabiat spent countless hours doing volunteer work at a Wildlife Recovery center near his home town in northern California. Finishing Grade 12 with a strong GPA, he enrolled in Biology at UC Davis and completed a Zoology Major with honours. A nature centre back home provided employment for a year, and it was during this time that he got the fateful tattoo.

When Chuck Tabiat decided to invest in his first tattoo, he did a lot of online research about local artists and the costs involved. He knew from the online reviews that Grant Jones was a stickler for realism, and he'd had his own studio for 12 years. Online he found a great male lion tattoo—the large head and mane of the King of the Jungle—and took it to show Grant, to get an estimate of the cost and the time. As it turned out, Grant had a similar image already in his Instagram portfolio—black with grey shading. It was a magnificent broad face and mane, peacefully gazing in one direction while the head of his female consort was shown underneath gazing in the opposite direction. Chuck couldn't afford both lions, so they agreed on the male only. That alone would cost $600 plus the tip. Chuck said he wanted the image on his torso. Grant smiled and counselled a more moderate approach. "How about saving your torso for when you're used to the feeling?"

"All right," Chuck conceded. "What about the back of my right hand?"

"Well," said Grant, "that's not a big enough area, and you could be disappointed with that in a few years because hands fade faster . . . maybe your forearm or your leg."

So Chuck agreed to his right calf. Two weeks later he had to lie face down for 5 hours on a bench in Grant's studio while the artist did the lion tattoo on the back of his leg. The process was quicker than Chuck had thought. Grant used his portfolio lion image with a thermo-fax to make a stencil. Then he applied a stick deodorant to help with the transfer. Chuck loved the purple image when he pulled away the stencil, so it was a 'go'. With his gloved hands, Grant rubbed a little A&D ointment on the design to help the needle slide along. Those first minutes were tough! He'd explained it already, that the machine drove needles in and out 80 to 150 times a second—fast enough not to puncture the skin and cause bleeding. Frequently Grant toweled the sore area. After an age, it seemed, he switched machines for shading, which went very quickly. The hot towel felt good, then it was picture time. Finally, Grant applied protective ointment and wrapped the leg in a bandage.

It seemed so long ago—just last spring. With the onslaught of summer heat, Chuck had to remember to keep it covered or wear sunscreen to keep it from fading. But the pain had long ago dissipated and he thought less about his tattoo as time went by.

He heard about a new type of zoo opening close to New York. He applied, was short-listed, then took the chance and paid for the flight to New York for the interview. The panel liked his résumé and appreciated his insightful questions about the new zoo concept.

Zoos are always going through changes—improvements to the sizes of enclosures, realistic settings, viewing accessibility, animal groupings. Changes reflect in some way what the public wants to see, what we think should be the offerings, the world of animals we would like our children to catch a glimpse of, to experience.

We would like visitors to see themselves as part of the great animal kingdom, included within the amazing diversity.

The interview panel explained to Chuck how the themes of diversity and inclusion had inspired a new concept in animal management to reflect an outlook more in touch with the times: a genderless zoo.

One director spoke for the Panel: "Animals have long been identified as male or female, but this runs counter to our new knowledge of human sexuality, now recognized to be a whole spectrum of possibilities, not limited by sexual organs. How could this be reinforced by what is on display at a zoo? To directly identify a zoo as 'genderless' is counter-productive, drawing attention to the aspect of gender; instead, the new zoo is termed a Species Only (SO) Zoo, avoiding any mention of male and female, focusing uniquely on the ***species*** characteristics and differentiation from ***other species***."

Chuck was fascinated. "Is that actually possible, when males and females are distinctly different?"

The director continued his explanation. "For years now the staff at the New York SO Zoo has been experimenting with blurring the distinctions between male and female birds and animals. Through careful genetic manipulation, we have been relatively successful at producing birds with less distinct male/female characteristics or a blend of the visual characteristics—colour, size, shape. Controlling and altering male/female behavior in animals has been more difficult. However, separating males and females has helped to increase a variety of blended behavior."

Chuck queried, "But would the offspring of the genetic changes carry on the changes, or would the offspring revert to natural differentiation?"

"A reasonable consideration," said the director. "Obviously, it requires more experimentation. But now for the question: Mr. Tabiat, are you interested in being part of our team?"

Chuck had been shown a salary schedule and was very impressed by the opening wages and benefits, plus the assurance of timely promotions. More important, he knew how difficult it was to find employment in his field of study. So his move to New York employment took place rapidly.

The SO Zoo outside the city had 800 animals representing 100 species. Admittedly, this was a small number of species compared to the Bronx Zoo with 650 species. With half the acreage of the Bronx, the SO Zoo opened only 50 acres to the Public. 40 acres were reserved for experimental genetic blending of genders and the other 40, referred to as "The Ark" by senior zoo employees, remained off limits except for designated staff.

Chuck spent his first 8 months tending to habitats in the 6 geo-regional areas for public viewing. In general this went without a hitch, until his supervisor discovered the tattoo. It was a beautifully hot day and Chuck had worn a new pair of cargo shorts. The tattoo showed beautifully and he was congratulating himself on how appropriate it was for this job when he was swiftly pulled aside by the supervisor, who was fuming.

"You realize that your tattoo shows a male of the species and the SO Zoo wants to de-emphasize dimorphism." Chuck hadn't heard the term since Wildlife Biology classes. He scrambled to remember: "di-" meaning "two", plus "morph" meaning "form", so "dimorphism" referred to obvious physical differences between the sexes. "You'd better wear long pants from now on. I'll lend you a pair for the rest of your shift."

The incident galled him, but he swallowed his pride, did his job faithfully, and collected the paychecks. Other than this, the first 8 months went by uneventfully, and his reliability and resourcefulness came to be appreciated.

Promotion came in the form of lab tech work in the experimental facility. But it was soon clear to his supervisor that Chuck's heart wasn't in the experimental work, and within a couple of weeks he was introduced to the work being done in the "inner sanctum", the Ark—work which might better suit him. Right away, on entering the Ark complex, Chuck was surprised to see animals as he was used to them—obvious males and females of every species kept at the zoo.

"But I was told that the whole idea of the zoo was to display species only, with no representation of genders within the species."

"That's true," his supervisor responded. "There is no conflict here because these animals are not on display."

"But why have them then?" asked Chuck.

"Ah," replied the super. "Well, we must maintain and have access to a healthy breeding pool for every species. The whole enterprise would die out without that. It remains unseen, but it is essential."

Chuck could see the sense in that and nodded slowly.

To his delight, he was allowed to wear shorts to work now, because his tattoo would not be seen by the public. Working with the African animal crew, he met a pretty young Kenyan woman named Grace Mwangi, whose experience on a Kenyan wildlife conservancy had netted her the job with the SO Zoo. Grace was an ebony beauty, clever, articulate and good-natured, and he fell for her immediately. At break times he learned about her background and university studies in Nairobi. They listened to each other's experiences and wondered at their common joy in working with the African cats. Grace admired Chuck's tattoo of the great maned lion and he explained how he had had to cover it when working in the public section of the zoo. Grace was indignant. Why on earth would they object to his impressive tattoo?

"My family doesn't go with tattoos," she said. "For one thing they don't show up well on our skin. But if I had one," she added vehemently, "it would be a lioness . . . to go with your lion." It took him by surprise, this warm support and closeness. He looked across at her then. She seemed to blush, although it was hard to tell beneath her beautiful dark skin. "Yes," she went on earnestly, "a lioness—and some cubs for my tattoo, if I had one". Then, out of the blue, "Chuck, could you come for dinner on Friday? I've been telling my parents about you and they'd love to meet you."

So work at the SO Zoo took on a different complexion for them both.

Months later, reflecting on their engagement, Chuck thought how naturally it had all come about. They had so much in common. In their work at the zoo, for instance, they both preferred the traditional vivid colours and familiar behaviours of the Ark animals. And they were both passionately committed to a breeding program.

The Sound of One Hand

Do you recall when LIRAA caught national attention? Left-handed people began to speak out; they became vocal about the history of injustices done to them from the dawn of civilization to the present. Every week, it seemed, there were fresh revelations about hardships endured by left-handed people in a right-dominated society. From the unavailability of left-handed scissors to the side of the road on which we drive, the prejudice of right-biased people was exposed for all to see. Even the words 'left' and right' demonstrated the issue: 'right' carried the connotation of 'correct', whereas the other was merely 'left' over.

Hubert was right-handed and had never really considered that being left-handed could cause problems for anyone. In part this was because his friend Joe had been a baseball phenomenon in high school with his left-handed pitching; many a visiting batter was scared spitless when the ball came out of nowhere at 85 mph! The school was proud of him. And Joe would say that baseball history is full of left-handed heroes like Lefty Grove or Sandy Koufax.

So Hubert was dumbfounded when he heard that a generation ago, even in Canada, left-handed elementary students had been forced to write with their right hands. He had never personally known any students who had been treated this way.

He read in the news that English gets its words 'gauche' and 'sinister' from French and Latin words for 'left-handed', where those same languages make right-handers come off sounding pretty good: 'adroit' and 'dexterous'. "That's not fair," thought Hubert, "Probably it's because right-handers weren't very good with their left hands and didn't trust people who were."

Valiantly, left activists declared "Left IS right!" and the movement took its name from the slogan. LIR Affirmative Action lobbied government for inclusion in the Charter of Rights and Freedoms: ". . . regardless of race, creed . . . manual preference". Activists argued that equality of opportunity alone would not redress imbalances; left-handedness had to be encouraged. In the States incentive programs were set up to award government grants to businesses which adjusted their hiring practices. To be ambidextrous was enviable; one qualified for either right-handed or left-handed positions in the job market.

But Hubert was not ambidextrous. He was part of the ho-hum, run-of-the-mill, oppressive right-handed majority, a 'handicap' in a society now acutely aware of wrongs perpetrated by past generations and determined to make up for that history. Hubert regretted being right-handed and he even apologized for it. Nevertheless, last August he had been displaced by a left-handed applicant for the position of school counsellor. The relevance of hand orientation eluded him until it was explained that the experience of being left-handed would place a counsellor in a better position for advising left-handed students. Despite Hubert's seniority, the union wouldn't defend him, so his job went to a recently graduated left-hander. The shop steward explained to him that their teacher union had had no choice; not to promote an available left-hander might have triggered all kinds of unhappiness.

At first Hubert was indignant, then depressed. "If 85 to 90 percent of the population is right-handed, others must be facing similar job losses," he thought. Perhaps he could open his own private practice as a counsellor, offering help to unemployed right-handers. If only society would recognize the stigma of being right-handed. Who knows? Those unemployed people might be suffering from a variety of injustices which, once known, would oblige employers to reach out to them.

That germ of an idea led Hubert to create DAEYVS (pronounced "daves"), an acronym for "Discover And Embrace Your Victim Status". As he explained on the website, people without work for whatever reason could come to him for consultation. He would help them to identify ways they had been victimized by society and steer them in a direction which could receive compensation, if not employment.

Almost immediately Hubert got a call and set up his first DAEYVS appointment. Brendon Chapman, a man about 45, had been replaced by a left-hander for driving a logging truck. Hubert welcomed this man to his basement office, listened to the details of his lost employment, then presented the DAEYVS program.

"From our phone conversation," he began, "it seems that you don't qualify for the more traditional victim categories. Is there anything you can think of from your own background which has given others an unfair advantage over you?" His client looked blank, so Hubert provided a prompt. "For example, did you grow up on a farm?"

Brendon was puzzled. "Why would that be a disadvantage?"

"Often farm life demands involvement of children for helping with chores, while urban families may provide their kids with time and opportunities to take lessons or to be involved in sports. There's a sophistication which goes with city living which gives urban youngsters an advantage over those growing up on a farm."

No, Brendon replied. He had not grown up on a farm.

"Well, then, on the flip side of that issue, you ***didn't*** have the wholesome experience of growing up with animals and nature.

That, too, is a disadvantage. In a sense, you were a victim of having to grow up surrounded by buildings."

The client looked dubious, so Hubert continued. "But let's explore another avenue. What birth order place did you have in your family? Were you the first, second, third, fourth child?"

"Why would that matter?" asked Brendon.

"From a counsellor's point of view, it makes all the difference. If you were the oldest child, you probably had to spend a lot of time looking after younger children."

"But I was the youngest," said Brendon.

"Then you suffered from being the last in the line-up. Your parents had given special attention to the first kids and didn't have the energy to devote to you. That qualifies—clearly you're a victim of birth order."

His client was skeptical. "What if I were the second or third among the kids in our family?"

Hubert responded matter-of-factly. "Then you would have no special treatment at all. That, too, would make you a victim of birth order."

"I don't see how this is helping," said Brendon. "How would this help with getting a job?"

"That's trickier," admitted Hubert. "We need to write up your approach to a job interview, highlighting your courage in spite of your circumstances to have come as far as you have in life, and stating your confidence in the employer's fairness to people who have struggled against huge obstacles."

Brendon was unconvinced, but paid the $80 consultation fee.

After his first client had left, Hubert took stock of how things had gone. Unfortunately, victim status would require a mass movement in order to get anywhere. He hadn't much hope of achieving the success of LIRAA.

Now, ***there*** was success! But you did need a large and very vocal group, like a class action law suit. You also needed publicity.

There'd been a sensational news item recently about a radical wing of LIRAA with communes in California and France, where only use of the left hand was permitted. In protest against a history of right dominance, the right hands were carried in slings. Work traditionally done with two hands was accomplished by two left-handed people working together.

Hubert sighed. Without having a group to broadcast your victim status, what hope was there for restitution? He considered his own situation and laughed ruefully, but with a little envy.

It was difficult now to imagine society before LIR Affirmative Action. For the remarkable changes wrought through their focus and vigilance, these people deserved applause. A thought struck Hubert and he grinned. Being sensitive to their feelings, he thought, we should restrict our applause to the sound of one hand clapping—the left, of course.

Reassessment

Lou counted himself lucky to have been born at just the right time in history. Across the country, universities were abuzz with a new vision for justice, reassessing the flawed record of past so-called 'achievements'—and he, Aloysius Johnstone, was participating in it!

Classes at Lou's university were cancelled on the first Monday of every month so that students could crowd into the gym for the Session. The meeting was run by The Committee of Public Safety, a group of 12 students who modelled themselves on the Committé of the French Revolution. For the assembly they wore the Revolution's famous red Liberty hats with red, white and blue cockades pinned on one side. At the very first Session it had been explained that the red Liberty hat originated with a similar hat called a pileus worn in Ancient Rome by slaves who had been freed. In the French Revolution over 200 years ago, that resonated with a country rejecting the tyranny of aristocracy. Now it connected with challenging and denouncing ignorant views of past generations.

Each Session began and ended with the attending crowd on their feet, loudly affirming 'Liberty! Equality! Fraternity!' To commence proceedings, a student from the audience would come to the podium microphone and read out a formal charge. By some stroke of luck, Lou's name was chosen for that honour of the opening Session. He remembered with a thrill reading out the charge, like throwing down the puck at the beginning of a hockey game. He was instructed to read the statement loudly, articulating clearly and speaking slowly, powerfully, so that the words would sink in.

"The Great Pyramid of Giza must be shunned by thinking people."

On the gym screens flashed a photo of the pyramid and a brief description was read out by the Session Moderator.:

"The Great Pyramid at Giza is the largest in the world, 146 metres tall, built with over 2 million stone blocks, each one weighing 2 tons or more. Herodotus said it took 20 years and 100,000 workers to build. It is a burial monument to King Khufu, who ruled in Egypt over 4500 years ago. "

The Moderator glanced behind him at the projected image of the Great Pyramid, then faced the audience again and solemnly declared, "I call the first prosecutor". He sat down on one of the chairs behind the podium beside two other figures seated in the line of chairs. One rose now and stood at the podium, grasping its corners and glowering at the audience. His face was lit by the stage flood lights.

"Khufu thought of himself as a god, and perpetuated that arrogance even in preparing his burial chamber. Can we imagine the enormous conceit of this tyrant, not content with ordering people around in his lifetime, but having them work for two decades after his death to create this monstrous burial mound? Here we are, 4500 years later, STILL paying homage to this bastard by visiting his tomb. I say, refuse to go there! Enough is enough!"

Members of the Committee who were seated in the first row began the cheering, clapping and foot-stomping.

The Moderator stood at the podium again and asked, "Do I hear a defense?"

Immediately a small group of four people appeared before the podium, dressed in gaudy tourist attire, with sunglasses, shorts, bright shirts, Tilley hats, carrying backpacks and holding up binoculars or clunky old-school cameras. They turned around, pretending to be at the pyramid site, snapping pictures and pointing at invisible features. One of them came to the podium mic and said loudly in melodramatic Oxford English, "Oh, it's so . . . grand, so . . . magnificent, so . . . awe-inspiring!"

Members of the Committee hooted with laughter and hollered, "Take them away!" Two capped members of the Committee pretended to arrest the tourists and hurried them down an aisle, while the tourists protested lamely with cries of "Let me take another picture!"

The Moderator declared, "These are the sort of clueless comments visitors have made for over 4,000 years. It's time to expose these monuments for what they truly are! I call the second prosecutor."

A young woman seated behind the podium came to replace the Moderator at the microphone.

"Imagine the wretched conditions of those who slaved away at cutting, transporting and lifting into place TWO MILLION blocks . . ." She paused. ". . . each the size of an SUV!" She paused again to let this sink in. "How can we possibly ENJOY visiting a place which would not exist except for the misery of 100,000 people?!" She repeated the figure. ". . . 100,000! What kind of unthinking, insensitive BRUTES must we be, to care so LITTLE about how this monument came to be? NO! We will REFUSE to visit it!" She paused once more dramatically, then asked the crowded gym: "What do YOU say? Do YOU approve of tyrants? Do YOU go along with slavery?"

Members of the Committee began a chant of "NEVER! NEVER! NEVER!" which was joined by various sections of the audience until most of the gym was shouting it out.

The Moderator held up his arm for silence. "You have a chance today to put feet to your decision. There are tables along the walls where you can sign petitions to the Egyptian government, travel agencies, consulates and embassies. AND we will petition our government to impose sanctions on Egypt if there is no move to stop tourism at the Great Pyramid. We WILL make a difference!"

There was applause from some in the crowd. Not to lose momentum, the Moderator indicated that all should rise for the motto, a resounding "Liberty! Equality! Fraternity!"

After signing a few petitions, Lou found his friend Parker in the crowd pouring out of the gym. Students were talking excitedly about the first Session and Lou insisted on treating his friend to chicken wings and a beer so that they could talk about the event. Parker agreed, but seemed oddly unimpressed by what had just happened.

At a pub table, as they waited for the plate of wings, Lou asked for his friend's impressions. Lynwood Parker was in his final year of the B.A. and Lou in his second. Not fond of his given name, Parker happily continued the tradition of his private school, where students called each other by last names. Lou had first met him in the Library, asked his help to navigate the stacks of books, and ended up enjoying a friendship.

Parker sipped his beer. "It was sort of fun, Lou." He hesitated. "But historically, they've probably got it wrong. Close to the pyramid is a village for the workers, and from the excavations, it seems unlikely they were slaves. What they created truly is incredible—and worth visiting. It's not about the Pharaoh, it's about the skills of the people who designed and accomplished it. You know that before building the Great Pyramid, the workers had to level the outside edge of many acres of the rock base, and they did that by digging trenches, and filling them with water to find and mark the level before cutting. Pretty clever! They made the four sides of the pyramid point north, south, east and west—with less than one degree in error—just by using the stars or shadows from rods. The place is amazing, Lou!"

Lou was surprised. "How do you know these details?"

"I'm planning a tour next summer of archaeological sites along the Nile," Parker explained, "and I've done a lot of reading already."

"Are you still thinking of going, after today?" asked Lou.

His friend laughed. "That little drama today doesn't change my mind. No offence to you, Lou—you were asked to read and you played your part well—but those guys didn't know much about what they were condemning."

Lou was stunned. "Will you go to the Session next month?"

"Sure!" said Parker. "It's amusing, anyway. Let's go together. Next time the beer and chicken wings are on me."

The second Session fell on Monday, November 1st. Anticipation of the event had built over the intervening month. Hilarity and curiosity were in the crowds which poured into the gym when doors were opened. Some sat, forgetting the protocol, but were reminded to rise by the solemn appearance of the Moderator. He looked different this time, wearing a black cape and a black bicorn hat with the red, white and blue cockade pinned on one side.

Parker smiled. "Apparently, he wants to look like Napoleon."

The moderator suddenly punched the air and shouted "Liberty!" The crowd loudly rejoined with "Liberty! Equality! Fraternity!" then noisily took their seats on the bleachers or the main floor rows of plastic chairs. When the noise had settled, the Moderator called out, "What is the charge?" A student seated close to the podium came to the mic and read:

"The Great Wall of China must be shunned by thinking people."

And so it went.

Afterwards, at the pub, Parker ordered a plate of chicken wings. Pints of beer came right away and as they sipped, Lou gave some of his own impressions.

"It's incredible, to think that 2 million people died in the effort to make the Great Wall of China!"

His friend agreed. "Yes! It was dangerous work in places. Life for the convicts must've been terrible. Not quite what we think of as doing community service, is it?" He grinned wryly. "But once again, the Committee today didn't give an accurate account. For one thing, Emperor Shi Huang didn't actually begin the wall; instead, he united existing walls to make a longer wall. Some of those original parts of the wall may have been around for 500 years before the Emperor. It took 6 different dynasties to complete the wall. And not everyone who worked on it was a slave; there were ordinary workmen, too. Also, there was a purpose for the wall. It wasn't just a tourist attraction. Primarily, the wall protected China from northern threats."

Chicken wings had arrived and Parker dug in. Lou looked incredulously at him.

"Ok, you can't tell me you know this because you're planning an archaeological tour of the Great Wall?!"

Parker laughed. "No, not this time! I cheated and asked one of the Committee members about their next target. When she told me it was the Great Wall, I had time to do a little research. I'd love to see it. One article said that rice was used in some construction because of its sticky, gluey quality. Who'd have thought of that?!"

Lou was unsure what to think. Rice used in the building process didn't much interest him.

"Should we be visiting any walled structures at all?" he asked. "It seemed to me she had a good point about North American cities having no walls. It's the distrust of past generations that led them to build walls."

"There's more to it than that," said his friend. "Actually, there ***are*** two older cities in North America which ***do*** have walls—Mexico City and Quebec City. Most newer cities were built at a time when walls were useless to protect against planes flying over and dropping bombs."

That hadn't occurred to Lou, and he sat sipping his beer. "So you'd want to see it?" he mused.

"When I was checking out pictures of the most interesting parts of the Wall, what stood out for me is an amazing mountain crest section of the Wall close to Beijing, but too steep for a lot of tourists. It's called Jiankou. Although the climb is a bit dangerous, that's where I'd like to explore watchtowers and take a sleeping bag for an overnight hike. Can you imagine it, Lou –sleeping on the Great Wall of China!"

"Send me a postcard," replied Lou, laughing.

The third Session fell on December 6th and was not as well attended because of term papers and the proximity to the Christmas break. Nevertheless, two-thirds of the gym filled up with students eager for the announcement of a new target. People were standing around talking when an air horn sounded. At the podium stood a figure less familiar, dressed in a red doctoral gown with three bars of black on each puffed sleeve.

"Is that our Chancellor?" asked Lou. "He's the only one on staff with a doctorate from Minnesota. That looks like his gown."

"It seems today the Moderator wants to look like the Chancellor." Parker smirked. "I didn't know you could rent those gowns—unless somehow he managed to persuade the Chancellor to let him borrow it for the day."

Lacking from the graduation regalia worn by the Moderator was a traditional mortarboard. In its place was Napoleon's black bicorn hat with a tricolor cockade pinned to it. The Moderator held his bicorn hat in the air by one corner and boomed out, "Liberty!" The crowd echoed back, "Liberty! Equality! Fraternity!" then took their seats on the bleachers and gym chairs.

"Today . . . " The Moderator stalled dramatically and looked around at his audience. "Today is a great day!" He paused again for emphasis. "We have looked at other cultures, other countries, but it is time to turn our attention to the appalling history of a ***Canadian*** icon!" There was a hush of uncertainty and expectation. "What is the charge?"

A student jumped to her feet and strode to the mic to make the announcement.

"The Canadian Pacific Railway must be denounced and shunned by thinking people."

Immediately there was talking mixed with laughter throughout the gym. On the giant screens appeared a CPR locomotive and dome train against the familiar backdrop of Rocky Mountains.

The Moderator raised his arm for silence.

"Many of us have been impressed by scenic pictures like this one of the train travelling by Lake Louise. In the 1880s the Canadian Pacific Railway was built across Canada, linking Montreal in the east to Vancouver in the west, a distance of 4700 kilometres. If we really knew the history of this railway, we would refuse to use it. I call the first prosecutor."

In his inimitable style, the first prosecutor positioned himself like a captain at the helm, grasping the corners of the podium and glowering at the sea of faces.

"Who would imagine the history of racism which mars this Canadian icon? More than 15,000 Chinese workers were brought by ship from California and from Southern China—cheap labour to help build the railway. They were given the most dangerous jobs, the most difficult terrain through the B.C. Rockies, and paid the least. It's said that one railway worker died for every mile of track between Calgary and Vancouver. To add insult to injury, in the famous "Last Spike" photo of 1885, all the Chinese workers were deliberately kept out of the picture. Would you ride a train which so abused—and killed—Chinese workers? NOT ME!"

He sat down, folding his arms defiantly. There was slow applause from the audience. The second prosecutor read from her sheet of notes, periodically glancing up.

"The Chinese workers had to handle nitroglycerin for blasting rock and tunneling. Hundreds died from accidents, harsh winter conditions, sickness and malnutrition. They were paid one dollar a day from which they had to buy food and clothing. Meanwhile, white workers were paid a dollar and a half to two dollars and a half and ***didn't*** have to pay for food or gear. Knowing how grossly unfair this was and the way they were treated by the CPR, can any one of us EVER ride that train track?"

Members of the Committee leapt to their feet, fists in the air. "NEVER! NEVER! NEVER!"

Several around the gym joined in. The Moderator was at the podium again.

"There is only one response to such a travesty of justice: DENUNCIATION! We denounce the Canadian Pacific Railway and everything it stands for!"

Members of the Committee hooted, hollered, whistled and clapped.

The Moderator raised his arm for quiet, then resumed.

"Today you have an opportunity to do something about racism. You can sign the petitions on these side tables—petitions to the provincial and federal ministers of tourism to shut down the CPR—and petitions to tourist agencies across Canada to denounce the rail company for this appalling history. Don't leave the gym without showing you care!"

It was a more subdued crowd which made its way from the gym, several signing the papers laid out on tables.

Once outside, Lou found his friend Parker. Neither of them felt like going to the pub. Parker admitted to knowing little about CPR history and suggested that they meet on Friday evening after the week's classes.

That Friday evening at 6 o'clock Lou found Parker already sitting at a table in the crowded pub. He had come with a friend, Monique, who Lou had met when she attended one or two theatre events with Parker. Monique was an Honour student who had come a year ago from Montreal to do grad studies with Dr. Warkentyne in the History Department. She had been the TA who helped mark undergraduate papers for a course Parker happened to be enrolled in. Monique had been impressed when Parker emailed appreciation of her comments on his paper, while gently challenging some of her criticisms. The challenging had annoyed her at first, but led to meeting for coffee and ended with laughter. She was clever, witty, petite but feisty, with a Latin spark that Parker found irresistible. The course had come to an end, and it was clear their friendship would continue.

Waiting for tacos, the three talked about current assignments and deadlines. Talk came around to the Monday Session and Parker introduced the topic so that Monique could easily join in.

"After last Monday, Lou and I decided to wait until now to discuss the Canadian Pacific Railway and what the Committee said about it. Over the past few days, I have checked online some of the prosecutor claims and I have to admit, it seems pretty bad for the CPR! Lou, I invited Monique to join us because she actually co-authored a paper on the building of the railway. So, tell us, Monique, is the Committee justified this time? Should we shun the railway?"

Monique pushed up the bridge of her moon-shaped glasses and settled back for an impromptu dissertation.

"You need to know a little background information first. In 1871 British Columbia agreed to become part of Canada, partly on condition that a railway would be constructed within the next ten years, linking the west coast to the east coast. Ten years went by and the federal government gave the contract for construction to the newly formed CPR.

"The government was concerned that the U.S. was expanding westward. So the race was on and people of many nationalities were hired: English, Italians, Swedes, Chinese. Considering the size of Canada, it makes sense that the workers arriving on the Pacific coast worked on the B.C. portion of the rail, whereas the Europeans began on the east coast. B.C. had the most difficult terrain. Almost all the workers who built the line from Vancouver to Craigellachie were Chinese. Often they were given dangerous work with the explosives to blast through rock, which could come hurtling out from the tunnels. It seems that workers across the country got the same lousy tents, and conditions could be difficult in other provinces, too. It's true that the Kicking Horse pass in B.C. was a killer to get the railroad through, but some say that the rock and muskeg of the Canadian Shield was almost as hard. There were places in Ontario where the tracks sank into bogs. In 1884 there were 4000 horses and 15,000 men struggling to complete the line and shoreline tunnels around Lake Superior.

"Chinese workers were certainly treated unfairly. The Chinese agreed to work for a dollar a day, thinking that would allow them to save money, but the wages were too low. You should know that a small house could be rented for $4.50 a month and the average salary at that time was about $1.50 a day. There was a real prejudice in Canada and opposition to bringing in Chinese workers, but Prime Minister John A. MacDonald said that either Canada used the cheap labour of the Chinese workers, or the railway wouldn't be built. So they came. And it's true that at least 600 Chinese workers died in the accidents and harsh winters with avalanches. Then, after the completion of the railway, Canada made it hard for Chinese people to immigrate by imposing an expensive head tax. All of that was racist and didn't end until after W.W.II."

Monique sighed, then continued. "Nevertheless, the CPR story does involve more than the unfair treatment of Chinese workers, and it's important to look at that. In the end, a hell of a lot of work by people of many nationalities over 4 years succeeded in completing a railroad to unite Canada. That rail line went on to help with immigration, transport of people and materials during the wars, and was a backbone for all kinds of development."

Having completed the history lesson, Monique finished her cider.

Lou sighed. "Would you yourself take the train to Banff, knowing what Chinese workers went through to build that line?"

"I don't think anyone's denying that the treatment of Chinese workers was wrong, but it would be crazy to throw away what all those workers across Canada strove to achieve. You know, Lou, I think most of the thousands of workers, including the Chinese, would have loved the opportunity to travel that line after it was finished. I have travelled the line all the way from Montreal to Vancouver already and the B.C. part is spectacular. Travelling that line doesn't mean you agree with everything that went into making it. But it would be insane to deny the value to Canada of the CPR."

Monique asked whether the next "target" had been disclosed. Maybe they could meet again after the January Session.

Lou looked worried. "The Committee is pretty good at stirring people up. It really is like the French Revolution!"

"I know what you mean," agreed Monique. "But these are early days. Not everything is going well for the Committee. The Status of Women has complained about the motto using the word 'fraternity', which comes from the Latin for 'brother'. They want a neutral word like 'comradery'. But the Moderator refused, saying that would spoil the connection with the French Revolution. Of course, he ***would*** say that; he's a man!" She grinned.

Parker laughed. "These things have a way of backfiring. I think the Moderator should check out what happened to Robespierre after he sent thousands to the guillotine; people decided he should get the same treatment!"

"I suppose," added Monique, "there might be some serious reassessment after that!"

Rumours about dissention within the Committee for Public Safety were never formally confirmed but student inquiries about cancellation of the next Session called for some response. Posters bearing the Committee seal, the tricolour cockade, appeared on campus bulletin boards, explaining that Sessions planned for the spring would be deferred until next fall. Apparently, the pressures of second term assignments were more demanding than anticipated.

Lou stood reading one of these posters in the Student Union Building. Beside him, reading the notice, Parker was amused and skeptical.

"Hey, Lou! I think that Robespierre just got the axe!"

"What do you mean?" asked Lou.

"Waiting until next fall means that some students will have graduated—they won't be around anymore. One of those is the Moderator."

All in the family

Force of Habit

Arthur Paynton talked to himself. Perhaps many of us do that, but in general we try to keep the conversation internal—you know, prevent our lips from moving or people might question our sanity. For Arthur, it began innocently enough with talking to God. In the nervousness of his day as a school teacher, Arthur found that he was thanking God under his breath for small blessings or for deliverance from one imminent disaster or another. "Thank you, Lord!" At first, it was a conscious thing, choosing to focus on the good things of each day rather than be dragged down by the irritations which arise in the pressure-cooker of teaching hundreds of students and dealing with administrative deadlines. "Thank you, Jesus!" When the photocopier was repaired and he could run off his handout—"Thank you, God!"

One of his colleagues chuckled, then remarked that she thought that was a great way to be—thanking God for every blessing. So Arthur was less concerned about being overheard and people noticed that Arthur frequently carried on a conversation without any obvious audience. "Lord—what do I do about this? Please show me what to do!" Talking to God out loud in the car was not a problem, since he would look like other people talking on their car phones.

Then Arthur and Meg bought a Goldendoodle puppy which required daily walks. Naturally enough, Arthur talked to Winston as he took him on leash around the neighbourhood. "Come along, Winston. Let's go!" One day he realized that he was saying something similar out loud to the vacuum cleaner as he dragged that around the house. Then, to his consternation, he found that he had actually spoken out loud to his shopping cart as he went down the aisles in Walmart. Worse, a woman had overheard him and smiled as she passed him in the aisle. Arthur determined to take himself in hand!

His aging father, living alone in an apartment, had chided him for not phoning more often. "There's no one to talk to. My voice gets rusty." Arthur thought ironically that would not be his own problem—unless he somehow managed to stop talking to himself.

Dealing with his own idiosyncrasy was much on his mind when he heard about Willy.

The school from which he had retired had suffered theft for many years—laptops, microphones, extension cords, a new microwave, even a hallway TV monitor. All of the stolen items were eventually discovered in a storage unit on the school property, placed there by Willy, one of the custodians. Arthur cast his mind back to the well-groomed, affable, grandfatherly man who enjoyed talking with staff and students. Willy was apparently a kleptomaniac, with no intention of selling or using the items he had taken. The excitement, the challenge of getting away with it was all he wanted. Arthur had suspected, but had said nothing, and now was relieved that he would not be part of deciding whether to prosecute. After all, everything had been retrieved and Willy was close to retirement. Arthur heard from former colleagues that Willy had been offered early retirement, but that he had refused, pleading to be kept on for two more years. Reluctantly, kindly, the administration had agreed.

The mobile home park where Willy lived was a short drive from Arthur's home. Thinking back on friendly after school chats with the custodian, Arthur paid a visit to Willy, who was delighted to see him again and happy to go for lunch at a local Tim Horton's. Over soup and a sandwich, Arthur inquired discreetly about how things were going and was thankful when Willy told him about the situation. He even volunteered information about one condition of his continued employment, that he would have to have counselling sessions arranged by the school board. These ended up being group sessions with others who had similar inclinations. No problem there, Willy said. He had made new friends and several of them met at The Horse and Rider for a beer on Thursday evenings. So Arthur felt reassured that his old acquaintance was dealing well with overcoming his weakness.

But that had not been the end of it. Smaller personal items belonging to staff began to disappear: a watch, two purses, a set of car keys. Willy swore he had nothing to do with it, and there was no proof that he was responsible for the latest thefts—until a student reported seeing him placing things in an unassigned locker. All the items were again accounted for and returned to their owners and Willy was told firmly that his employment was terminated.

Arthur phoned and arranged to meet for lunch again. Over the meal he told Willy about his own tendency to talk to himself and some of the funny situations which had occurred. Arthur thought that might open the way for Willy to share what had happened. He needn't have been concerned. The custodian frankly admitted everything which had led to being fired.

"But they won't stop me from dropping in for visits at the school cafeteria. They'll allow that."

"Are you still meeting with your counsellor?" asked Arthur.

"No, there's no need. But the group still meets on Thursdays. It means a lot to me." That sounded positive. Arthur wished Willy a good week, and left for home.

School news sifted down to him via the grape vine of former colleagues. Barely a month had gone by before students complained of losing items from their lockers: an expensive set of

Bosch headphones, a silver flute just recently purchased by parents for their daughter's band class, a new ski jacket. School policy was to encourage trust and honesty by forbidding use of locks on student lockers. Clearly, that had not worked. Suspicion fell immediately on Willy, who dropped in to visit with staff in the cafeteria at least once a week. A hallway camera helped to identify the culprit, showing Willy just after the lunch bell, surreptitiously taking a bag from one locker and deftly slipping it into a little used broom closet. So the hoard of stolen items was discovered and police were called in this time.

"I used to worry about being caught," Willy confided to Arthur. "But the group has helped me to see this for what it is. All of us have been this way for as long as we can remember. It's just the way we're built, and it's wrong for people to try to change that. It's a great group. You'd like them, Art. Like you talking to yourself—who cares? You might find we have a lot in common."

Arthur didn't think the situations were similar, but didn't say so.

"You could go to prison," he protested.

"You know, Artie, I don't think it would stick. Most things get returned in the end, so what's the big deal? It feels right to me and that's what counts. My lawyer says I have a right to the pursuit of happiness, just the same as anyone else."

Most of the lunch crowd at Tim Horton's had left. Apparently remembering an engagement, Willy glanced up at a clock on the restaurant wall behind Arthur.

"Can you see the time, Artie? I don't have my glasses."

Arthur turned and checked the clock time. "A quarter to two."

"I'd better get going," said Willy, and hastily said goodbye.

Arthur was in no rush, and sat meditatively sipping the last of his cold coffee. Perhaps Willy was right; what business was it of anyone to try to change the way he was? Maybe people were just born that way.

Then he remembered the photos of his Goldendoodle which he had intended to show Willy, who liked dogs. Absent-mindedly, he patted his pockets for his cell phone and recalled that he had put the phone between them on the table. So when Willy had asked him to check the clock time . . .

Arthur sighed heavily and held his head in his hands.

"Damn!" he muttered. Then, "What do I do now, Lord?"

He realized that a couple at another table had overheard and were looking curiously at him. Arthur smiled self-consciously and rose to go.

"Just saying a quick prayer," he told them. The woman's response was unexpected and unequivocal.

"That's a great habit!" Pointing to a table, she asked, "Is that yours?"

On a table by the exit was his cell phone!

"Thank you, Jesus!" Much relieved, Arthur picked it up and noted the distance from where he had been sitting. Had Willy thought . . . ? It didn't matter. He had his phone back.

"Thank you, God!" he said aloud again, then turned to thank the couple for drawing his attention to it. They must have just left.

Essentials

On a warm spring morning, Arthur sat at the kitchen table, gazing contentedly out at daffodils in the garden, marveling at the warm amber glow on the trunk of a birch tree. Shortly after Arthur's retirement, the passing of his father and then unexpected deaths of friends were causing him to think more about his own mortality. What help might he give to others while he still had strength and health? How could he set his own house in order so that a heart attack or other surprise would not leave others to sort through a mess of paperwork and unnecessary items? Meg had boxes of loose photos from the years before digital photo collecting. She despaired of ever getting these memorabilia into family photo albums, and Arthur joked that there was no need for her to worry; when she was buried, he would throw the photos in with her.

On this beautiful Spring morning, Arthur sat thinking about how he would inevitably die without ever understanding many of the things which made up his material world: how glass, plastic or metal are made; all the processes involved in producing cars, jets, computers, TVs, cell phones, the Internet, even Zoom conferences. These last had become really important for communication when COVID 19 hit, when people were warned to stay at home as much as possible. That too had caused Arthur to think about his own mortality.

Fear of contracting the Coronavirus had some curious effects. Arthur noticed, on his first weekly trip for groceries, how traffic drove more slowly, the cars maintaining an extra car-length of distance on the road, giving a wider berth to the occasional bike riders—a spin-off from "social distancing". In a parking lot for a local high school, the few cars there were parked in every other stall with one car space left vacant in between. At the grocery store Arthur dutifully wore his mask, but it continually fogged up his glasses, so he was regularly pulling it aside to de-fog. He was yelled at by an employee who noticed him pushing his shopping cart past another shopper who had stalled indecisively in an aisle. Arthur had tried to keep his distance and to be considerate, but maintaining a 6 foot buffer seemed impossible unless one waited for others to make up their minds. There were arrows on the floor to keep the flow of traffic in one direction only. Some shoppers got around this by backing up until they could get into another aisle with no obstructions.

Occasionally someone coughed and heads turned to look with suspicion at the culprit. Suspicion because people could be asymptomatic—carrying the deadly virus but unaware of it, not affected by it themselves—or pre-symptomatic, infected but not yet experiencing the symptoms. But if symptoms surfaced, if someone coughed or sneezed, well then, COVID was lurking in the shadows and death might be imminent, not only for the cougher, but potentially for anyone who happened to be within earshot.

Yes, life hung by a thread when the enemy was invisible and apparently killing millions around the globe. Well, thousands anyway. People in retirement homes were particularly susceptible, their bodies more vulnerable with aging. It was called "comorbidity", meaning there was already something seriously wrong with one's health. Meg was beginning to suffer from arthritis in one knee. She told Arthur that might be the thin edge of the wedge. She might be rushed to hospital tomorrow, gasping for a respirator, and it would be just her luck that the last one had been assigned minutes before to a previous patient. Just thinking about it brought on a dry cough.

"Let's not call for the undertaker yet," Arthur chided. "The number of quick recoveries is amazing."

Meg was not buying it. "Look at the hotspots of the world—Korea, Spain, Italy, New York, Brazil . . . . People are dropping like flies!"

Arthur sighed. "Of course the news is going to report the worst. But when they tell us how many contracted COVID today, do they also tell us about the numbers for other life-threatening illnesses? And when they tell us how many died, do they tell us how many of those were already really sick with something else?"

Secretly, Arthur was uneasy about Meg's diabetes; getting COVID 19 might be as dangerous for her as the news reports made out. So they followed the rules about distancing and stayed home as much as possible. Arthur did the shopping only when necessary.

Back in March, their friends Henry and Donna had intended visiting an elderly aunt who had fallen and broken her leg, but the visit was put off indefinitely when they realized that they might unknowingly carry the virus into her apartment. Henry told him, "Her life could be cut short and our thoughtlessness might be responsible." Arthur remembered that the aunt had recently celebrated her 98th birthday. He wondered, how could death at 98 be considered cutting a life short? Wouldn't it be better to have the warmth of a family visit and risk the loss of a few months of life?

And then a glimmer of a new thought occurred to him, something he couldn't share for weeks with anyone—not because he felt he had to keep it secret, but that he couldn't see how to adequately articulate it. What was the use of people anxious to stop physical sickness and death, when they weren't equally concerned about spiritual survival? And that, too, involved an invisible enemy. He wondered whether the world would ever unite to combat spiritual evil, whether even one country would shut down business as usual, risking economic ruin, in order to stem the tide of a spiritual pandemic.

On Vancouver Island, where they intended to move soon, the tide had turned and businesses were opening up again. All major stores were operating and several restaurants were serving tables again. Whale-watching and kayak lessons were back in swing for the tourist season. Even in Langley, Meg was able to arrange a hair appointment and pedicure. The library hadn't re-opened yet and churches remained shut. But as Meg sensibly pointed out, at least essential services had resumed.

Paintings and Crabs

In retirement, Arthur and Meg Paynton moved from the lower mainland to Courtenay on Vancouver Island. It was a dream come true—for Meg, the beauty of the Comox Valley; for Arthur, the joy of salmon fishing. Meg could also visit her reclusive brother who lived in a cabin not far from Cumberland. But mostly, it meant living close enough to their son Pete and his wife Rachel, so that their grandson could drop by for lunch or after school. It was the chance of a lifetime to build a relationship, to watch Patrick growing up, and even have a hand in raising him. Not always easy, but in the end, deeply satisfying. Take last week, for example.

On Monday afternoon, the front door banged open and the loud, angry voice of eleven year old Patrick preceded him.

"It's ***SO*** frustrating!"

He burst into his grandmother's living room, kicked off his canvas hi-tops, flung his backpack on the couch and flung himself beside it. Grandma Meg emerged unruffled from the kitchen with a bowl of chips and a can of root beer which she placed on the glass table in front of him, taking a seat opposite. Patrick was so worked up he didn't greet his Nana with the usual hug or acknowledge what she had brought out. Absent-mindedly, he popped open the can, took a gulp, then continued with the story of his day.

"You do a ***favour*** for someone and you get ***screwed***!"

Meg kept her voice calm. "What happened?"

"There's a kid named Manny who can't draw, so I drew his map for him. He labelled the cities and rivers, but I drew it. And when he passed it in, he told the teacher."

"Really? He told her that you drew it? That's odd. Do you know why?"

"Manny's family comes from Kenya. He ***always*** tells the truth. He says that in Kenya the teacher would be ***pleased*** that students are helping each other. Just my luck, Smitty didn't see it that way. She kept me in at lunch and gave me a lecture."

"So what was Mrs. Smith concerned about?"

"She said it wasn't honest—that she'd almost given Manny a mark he didn't deserve because he didn't draw his own map. But Manny told her the truth, so I can't see what's the big deal."

Meg thought for a moment. She liked the approach of the Kenyan teacher, but didn't think saying so would help her grandson's respect for Mrs. Smith.

"Well, maybe it's important for Manny to try to draw the map himself." She added hastily, "but it ***IS*** hard to be reprimanded when you were trying to help."

Her grandson scowled. "You and Papa always say, "What goes around comes around. Treat people right and they'll treat you right. But it doesn't really work that way, does it?"

Patrick knew she would bring up Christian faith, so he added, "Even if Jesus said it."

Meg sighed. "No, it doesn't always turn out, that when you are kind to others, things will work out well. Sometimes what happens is unfair. But Jesus said something different. He said, "Love your neighbour the way you love yourself." He didn't promise it would work out well. Nevertheless," she continued in her own defense, "it often does work out that people respond with kindness when we are kind to them."

"But not always, so it isn't true. What you told me isn't true." Patrick looked at her accusingly. "I used to believe that, but I'm older now." Averting her eyes, he glanced over, as he often did, at the painted scene of their town and the distant glacier. His grandmother followed his gaze.

"I really like that painting, too," she said. "Remember how you commented on how well the artist did the forest patches below the glacier? And you ***would*** notice that, because you're so good at sketching. But it's not as good as a photo, is it?"

"It isn't ***supposed*** to be a photo," replied Patrick. "It doesn't have every detail, but it's fantastic!"

Meg continued. "What if I said that the painting isn't ***right*** because a lot of the details are missing? In fact, some of the roads and houses in the painting don't really look like that. ***You're*** an artist—how would you answer that?"

Patrick rose to the occasion. He sounded older than his eleven years.

"I'd say it doesn't matter, because the painter did the picture so well that you recognize the glacier and you know where it's meant to be. She got the main things right."

"Oh . . . so you could say that the painting accurately represents our glacier even if some details in the town are wrong?"

"Yeah—I guess."

"Ok, well, we told you that if you treat people right, they'll treat ***you*** right. That's often the way it works out, so in general it's true, even if you can find some exceptions."

Meg tried to change the focus. "Manny is an unusual name."

Patrick was relieved to talk about something else. "His real name's Emmanuel. But everyone calls him 'Manny'—even his sisters," he added, in case Grandma Meg might think Patrick was making fun of Emmanuel. "The only one who calls him 'Emmanuel' is his Mum when she picks up the kids after school."

"Emmanuel is a great name. It means 'God with us.'"

"Yeah, I know—he told the class. It's kind of funny for Manny, though. He's great in soccer, but ***sucks*** in everything else." Patrick snorted. "Not exactly 'God with us'!"

Meg was silent for a moment. "In an odd way, maybe Manny's weaknesses are good for other people."

Her grandson wasn't really curious, but he was polite. "What do you mean?"

"That God is giving to people around Manny an opportunity to help him. And when people do that, they end up being blessed."

"I don't ***think*** so!" retorted Patrick, his anger flaring up again. "I helped him today and Mrs. Smith chewed me out for it! I sure didn't get blessed!"

"It doesn't look like it," Meg conceded. "But keep on helping—just don't do his school work for him . . . and you ***will*** be blessed, in the end," she added.

Patrick wanted to set the record straight about his friend.

"Actually, he's pretty good with building things. We're buddies for a science fair project on catapults. I'm designing the poster, and Manny's making a working model. It looks pretty good already."

"Sounds great! I'd like to see it. When's the Science Fair?"

"Friday afternoon in the gym." Patrick was finishing off the bowl of chips. He looked up at his grandmother. "I wish they weren't poor. Manny's family is really poor. Everything they have is second hand." He continued bitterly, "Jesus said, 'Blessed are the poor', but that's not true, is it? Life is really hard for them."

Meg sensed his heaviness. "Is anyone helping them?" she asked.

"Yeah. Their church helps with meals and baby-sitting. Some other things, too. It's still tough."

She nodded and was quiet for a while. "You know, Patrick, Jesus actually said, 'Blessed are the poor ***in spirit***—those who ***know*** that they are poor, because that can lead to asking God for help. And everybody's poor in that way—we all need God in our lives, but not all of us ***know*** that we're poor."

"Thanks for the pop," he said suddenly. "Gotta go."

Meg and Arthur attended the Science Fair. They spent time in front of each display to hear students explain their projects: the grade 4 volcano which had erupted baking soda and vinegar all over a table; a lemon battery no longer powering a flashlight, but being used by students trying unsuccessfully to zap each other; paper airplane designs which were still being flown across the gym for the longest flight. Grade 5s had more sophisticated displays showing how a reflecting telescope works, and an experiment comparing conductors and insulators. Grade 6s had a working worm farm and a display board diagram of the strata. Then there was the magnificent catapult, built and demonstrated by Manny, while Patrick retrieved projectiles— frozen peas and bits of eraser. Manny generously allowed Patrick's grandparents to try out the catapult. Lots of people jockeyed to be next to try it, so Meg and Arthur moved on.

Technically, the purpose for their visit was over. They could see that kids in the Grade 7 section were standing by their displays, but had few visitors. Meg nudged Arthur, who glanced at his watch, but good-naturedly moved to look at the Grade 7 displays. These focused on the theme of Oceans, with some students demonstrating water desalination, others manning a chart of plastics and ocean pollution. A giant wall chart showed the different ocean zones and layers. Meg stopped before a poster about crabs. Pictured was a Japanese Spider Crab, 12 feet across from tip to tip! Meg was particularly intrigued by a written explanation of how a crab molts, or sheds, its carapace in order to grow a larger shell.

For her husband, who had forgotten his glasses, she read aloud, "When a crab gets bigger, it grows a new soft exoskeleton under the old shell, then swells with water to cause a crack in the old shell and the crab with its new shell carefully backs out of the old one, a process of several minutes, sometimes over an hour. This molting happens 6 or 7 times in the first year, then once or twice a year after that. In this way, each molt can allow the crab to grow 15 to 25% in size. After the molt, for a couple of days the crab is very vulnerable until the new shell hardens."

Arthur was becoming restless; the hockey game would be on at five and he wanted to hear the pre-game commentary. Reluctantly, Meg agreed to leave. "It would have been nice to have a few more minutes," she told her husband, "I was enjoying learning about a few things," and added pointedly," but it ***was*** generous of you to give ***some*** time to your grandson."

Meg had seen enough to think over how similar people are to crabs—spiritually.

She tried to explain her idea to Arthur as they drove home. She related the Monday conversation she had had with Patrick.

"The faith that you have as a child has to grow to accommodate your new understanding as a teenager, then again as an adult. And at that time when your new larger 'shell' is replacing the smaller one you had, you're vulnerable. Others can come along and tell you that big crabs don't need shells; shells are just for little guys. But they'd be wrong, because no matter how big they get, crabs need shells. As their inside bodies grow, what covers them has to be replaced with a carapace large enough to protect the larger crab. Our own faith grows to make sense of new knowledge, experience—and reflection."

She was conscious of having talked a lot while her husband drove without speaking, so she paused now and waited for him to express his own thoughts. But he didn't reply and she wondered whether she might have said too much.

They parked the car and as they walked toward the house, Arthur looked deep in contemplation.

"What do you think?" asked Meg.

"Well . . ." began Arthur sheepishly, "I was trying to remember whether tonight is the last playoff game for L.A. and Chicago."

Meg shook her head in disbelief. Had he even ***tried*** to follow what she was saying? She could feel her anger mounting, but kept silent.

As soon as the door closed behind them, Arthur flopped down on the couch and reached for the remote. Meg wandered into the kitchen, from where she could hear the voice of a hockey commentator.

Oh, well. There had been a time when Arthur was unwilling to attend ***any*** school function. Thank God at least ***that*** had changed! She realized that she was thinking differently about changes—in Patrick, in Arthur, in herself. And she reflected with sadness that growing a new shell is a lonely process; each crab molts in its own time, when it's ready.

Uncle Sid's Legacy

All of Pete's teaching career took place in the Comox Valley. Until his own parents, Arthur and Meg, retired and moved to Courtenay from the mainland, Pete was the closest family member to eccentric Uncle Sid, who lived as a recluse in a lakeside cabin beyond Cumberland. For those many years before Pete's parents made the move, his mother Meg would inquire every other month whether Pete and his family had been out to visit her brother at the cabin. No matter how subtly she mentioned this over the phone, it was clearly a concern and an expectation. At first, Pete drove out to Cumberland by himself to visit his uncle. Then, when Pat was about grade 3, his Mum and Dad would drive out with him occasionally on a Sunday afternoon to take a pie and visit Great Uncle Sid. They did invite Sid over to their own house for special dinners, but he would politely decline. Pies and ice cream delivered to his door were another matter.

As the adults talked in the cabin kitchen, Patrick was left to explore three rooms which could only be negotiated by narrow passages through high stacks of books and magazines. Sid was a pack rat, collecting every set of World Book or other encyclopedia discarded by schools as they updated or went digital. Many of the stacks had remained the same since Pete and his sister Tabi had been there as kids. Maps and charts gleaned from old National Geographics were thumb-tacked to the cabin walls. Most intriguing for Patrick, however, was an enormous butterfly collection in a glass display case and another display case with spiders from around the world.

Sid had had a career as an entomologist in Zaire before it reclaimed its previous Congo name. Having studied entomology in Brussels, he was fluent in French, an asset for getting the job in Zaire.

Patrick often asked about the specimens in the glass cases and received some pretty specialized knowledge as a result. He learned that spiders are not insects because they have eight legs, not six. Stranger still, they have eight eyes, not the two compound eyes of flies.

"So why did you study them, if they're not insects?" asked Patrick when he was eight years old.

Uncle Sid explained that entomologists study arthropods, not just insecta, and Patrick nodded even though he didn't understand. Sid had never had children. But Patrick could intuit what an arthropod might be since Uncle Sid immediately took him to see the aquarium with a live scorpion which he fed on crickets. Pat once watched for half an hour in a darkening room while the scorpion, tail raised but immobile, waited for the right moment to catch a cricket. Pat's vigil came to an end when he was called to the table for pie and ice cream, only to discover that while he and the family were consuming pie, the cricket had also been consumed. Disappointing, not being a witness.

Sid sensed that Patrick was genuinely interested in how and where all the specimens had been obtained, so he did something he had rarely done with Peter and Tabi when they had visited him as children. He told Pat stories about his time in Zaire, with Pat's parents listening in. Perhaps it was in part that Sid was aging and the memories would soon die with him. He described how he had gone as a young scientist to the Congo River to study the spread of malaria through the Anopheles mosquito. From a high shelf

Sid took down plastic models of mosquitoes as large as birds and showed for comparison actual tiny specimens from his microscope slide collections. They looked as small as the lead in the end of a pencil.

Sid had gone in 1971 from his university studies in Brussels to a research job in Leopoldville, shortly after renamed Kinshasa. As Sid explained to his family, just before 1900, King Leopold II of Belgium had exploited the Congo for rubber and ivory, killing people who didn't keep up with the quotas. It was brutal. Small wonder that in 1971 General Mobutu decided to change the name of the capital from Leopoldville to Kinshasa. He began a program called "Authenticity" to rid his country of European names. The name of the country itself had been chosen by the Portuguese 400 years ago when they had named the area 'Congo' after the Kongo people whom they encountered. General Mobutu replaced that Portuguese choice with 'Zaire', from "nzadi", an ancient Kikongo word for "river". Ironically, "Zaire" was the Portuguese version of this word! Anyway, it shouldn't have mattered; both names, Congo or Zaire, are rooted in the region. Joseph Mobutu renamed himself "*Mobutu Sese Seko Nkuku Ngbendu Wa Za Banga*". An Internet search will likely tell you this means, "The omnipotent warrior who goes from victory to victory, leaving a trail of fire." Sid, who knew Lingala, said it really translates as, "The only rooster in the farm who will remain for a long time". Hmmm—that doesn't sound quite the same, but Sid said it's a matter of interpretation. In the context of the culture, the rooster image conveys the same idea. With all the self-aggrandizement of that lofty title, you'd think people would have smelled a rat, but they didn't. For 32 years Mobutu ripped off millions of dollars given by the U.S.. For weekend shopping trips, he would take the Concord jet to Paris. So the Congo suffered—from Europeans, yes, but also from their own. "*Mobutu Sese Seko Nkuku Ngbendu Wa Za Banga*". Sid said it again. He liked rattling it off.

"I kept to myself," explained Sid. "As long as I regularly reported on malaria and recommended how to deal with the mosquitoes, they left me alone."

"What exactly did you study?" asked Rachel, partly to help her son Patrick understand the conversation.

"First of all, you have to understand that not all mosquitoes bite animals. We know now that there are hundreds of species of Anopheles, but only about one in five is a vector for malaria. *Anopheles gambiae* is the species responsible for the spread of malaria. We tried to learn more about how the mosquitoes spread malaria, and why people in the center of the city were ten times less likely to be infected. There are almost 2 million deaths from malaria every year, most in sub-Saharan Africa and most of those kids younger than 5 years old."

"How can you tell a poisonous mosquito from other mosquitoes?" asked Patrick.

To help explain, Sid pulled down the brown plastic model as big as a robin. "When an Anopheles mosquito lands on a surface, it tilts its head down with a 45 degree angle in its back. Other mosquitoes rest with their bodies parallel to the surface. But they're not poisonous, Patrick. When they suck in blood which is contaminated with parasites, the parasites multiply in the gut of the mosquito, then get into the spit—the salivary gland, all set to inject into the next human from which blood is sucked."

"What makes that area so bad for mosquitoes?" asked Rachel. "Is it the rainfall?"

"No," replied Uncle Sid. "Actually, the Comox Valley gets more rainfall than Kinshasa. It's the year-round heat and humidity, plus all the swampy areas beside the river—perfect for mosquitoes." He pointed to an old wall map. "This 35 kilometre stretch of the Congo River is called the Malebo Pool, and right beside it is the capital city of Kinshasa with over 13 million people. It was about one and a half million when I arrived, back in 1971. It's grown like crazy, the third biggest city in Africa."

"What a dumb place to build a city, right beside a huge mosquito area!" commented Peter. "Why on earth would people live there?"

"Well, it seems strange to us," said Sid, "but you can't use boats on the Congo River to navigate the Livingstone Falls, just below Kinshasa. The 300 kilometres to the ocean are blocked off by the Falls. But going inland to Kisangani, about a thousand kilometres, is great after the Malebo Pool. That's why the city of Brazzaville is also there, on the north shore, facing Kinshasa. I guess people thought river travel was more important than mosquitoes."

"All right," said Peter. "Then how can they get rid of the mosquitoes? There's got to be a way to wipe out mosquitoes. We used to kill mozzies in the tire swings just by putting a little bleach in the water. With 2 million deaths a year, we should look at worldwide extermination of these blood suckers!"

"NO!" Uncle Sid snapped angrily and glared at Peter. "You don't know what you're saying! They're an important part of the ecosystem and have to be protected, not eradicated!"

Rachel protested. "But, Uncle Sid, you studied malaria in Kinshasa and you saw the children die. What possible good comes of these mosquitoes or of any mosquitoes?"

Sid glowered and pushed his mosquito models back on the high shelf. He seemed to be trembling with anger, trying to control it before he responded.

"Over 90% of mosquitoes don't suck blood. Even in the species which do, it's only the females. You probably don't know that mosquitoes also pollinate flowers. Catfish depend on the larvae for food. People eat the catfish. Mosquitoes are part of the diet for all kinds of creatures—fish, frogs, lizards, birds. And thanks to the Anopheles mosquitoes and the Livingston Falls, Portuguese slave traders had a hard time going up the Congo River. That's a very good thing! If you mess with nature, you don't know the terrible things you could unleash!"

He was red in the face, arms folded in defiance. Peter thanked him for showing them the models and explaining so many interesting things, then they hugged him and left for home.

After Patrick had gone to bed, Peter and Rachel discussed their afternoon visit to Uncle Sid.

"I'd forgotten how touchy he can be," said Peter. "Mum told me once that he has some weird notion that whatever happens to mosquitoes is like what happens to a canary in a coal mine; it's the penultimate test for the well-being of the planet!" They both laughed.

Patrick, however, was fascinated. On pie delivery days, he never tired of asking questions about Uncle Sid's experiences in the DRC and Sid was obviously happy to have a receptive audience. He showed Pat some light-coloured clothes he had worn to lessen the chances of being bitten and the mosquito netting which he had used back in the '70s. He showed his great nephew photos of a climb up Mount Nyiragongo, a jungle trip to see gorillas, and his flight to Kisangani, from where he took a three week barge trip back to Kinshasa along the Congo River. Tropical forest and riverside huts dominated the pictures.

Visiting Uncle Sid became a highlight for Patrick. This was mutual, a pleasant surprise to Sid's sister Meg when she heard about the growing friendship. Pat's grandparents, Meg and Arthur, had recently moved to Courtenay from the mainland and were busy setting up their new home.

From his parents Patrick found out when Sid had a birthday and planned something special. In Pat's favourite movie, 'Jurassic Park', scientists discover a prehistoric mosquito trapped in amber. It had sucked the blood of dinosaurs whose DNA could then be extracted to bring to life again Tyrannosaurs, Velociraptors, and a whole host of extinct reptiles. The mosquito connection got

Patrick thinking. He talked his idea over with his father, Peter, and the two of them found on the Internet a site selling replicas of the Jurassic Park amber bearing a trapped mosquito. They also came across a National Geographic article describing an unbelievable find in Montana oil shale: a 46 million-year-old fossilized mosquito with traces of blood showing up. The DNA had not survived. But Pete printed the article and Pat wrapped it up with the paper weight amber replica which they ordered from Amazon. Uncle Sid was delighted with the birthday gift. Peter took a photo of him with one arm around Patrick's shoulders, the other holding up the amber globe.

Sometime after Pat turned 13, during a visit to the Cumberland cabin, Patrick brought up again the topic of malaria mosquitoes. "How many eggs do the females lay? Are they like female flies, laying about 500 eggs?" he asked.

Uncle Sid smiled. "Not quite, Pat! The female lives for about 2 months and can lay as many as 5,000 eggs during that time. The males, which do not bite humans, only live about a week."

"Uncle Sid," asked Patrick carefully, "Isn't there some way to stop the females from spreading malaria?"

Sid described to him a new method for eradicating unwanted insects. A professor at Oxford, Dr. Luke Alphey, had written a paper on RIDL, short for 'Release of Insects carrying Dominant Lethals,' supposedly a non-toxic way to get male mosquitoes to infect and kill off the female larvae.

"Great!" said Patrick enthusiastically. But Uncle Sid was cautious. It involved genetic modification.

"I don't trust them. It's a plot," he said, "probably part of the same group that's pushing for hydroelectric plants on the Congo River. You know, Pat, when Tennessee brought in hydroelectric dams back in the 1930s, they killed the malaria by killing the mosquitoes."

"But isn't that a good thing?" asked Patrick, innocently.

"If you've got quinine and chloroquine, you don't need hydroelectric dams and you sure as heck don't need GMO," stated Uncle Sid. "You just use what's naturally available, like rubbing your skin with oil that has lavender, peppermint, basil, or eucalyptus in it. You stay away from the worst areas before dawn and after dusk. You know, South Africa would like nothing better than to create a huge hydroelectric dam bigger than China's Three Gorges Dam—just below Kinshasa. Now you tell me, Pat, when another country wants to dam the Congo River, there's something fishy going on. The truth is, they'd wipe out fish species and kill off mosquitoes."

"But killing off the Anopheles is good, isn't it?" asked Patrick again.

"No, sir! It's not natural. And it's a plot to control the mineral wealth of Africa, the uranium and copper. I suspected as much when the Inga Dam was built in the '70s. You mark my words, Pat. When they wipe out the mosquitoes, the end of civilization as we know it is just around the corner."

Sid could tell the boy was listening closely, so he continued.

"There's been thousands of years of abusing creation instead of caring for it. And what's happening now with trying to eradicate the mosquitoes—it's the final straw before we see some of those terrible scenes in the Revelation."

Patrick conveyed all of this to his parents, who tried to bring some moderation to Sid's views without completely destroying their son's admiration for him.

Two years later, when Sid died unexpectedly from an aneurysm, Patrick joined his parents and grandparents in sorting through Sid's lifetime accumulation of books and magazines. Most encyclopedias and books from Sid's cabin were declined by local libraries and even by Thrift stores, so ended up being taken to paper recycle bins.

The aquarium and glass display cases transferred to the Payntons' basement where Patrick could enjoy them. He was thrilled with the plastic models of mosquitoes, as well as the microscope slide collection, which he showed to his Grade 10 science teacher, Mrs. Miller, after school one day the following week. She had her Master's degree in microbiology, and was the ideal person to enthuse over his new treasures. Her opinion meant a great deal to Pat. Mrs. Miller listened attentively while he described Uncle Sid's distrust of genetically modifying the male Anopheles mosquitoes to pass on a lethal element to female larvae. And she listened to the explanation of why hydroelectric dams might harm the Congo River. Then Patrick asked, "But what do ***you*** think about his ideas?"

She paused to consider how best to reply. "First of all, Patrick, we need to acknowledge that your Uncle Sid was a remarkable man and a scientist to respect. That does not make him right about everything. It's a very good thing to be cautious about 'messing with nature', and to look at all the options. Having said that, I think the hydroelectric dams would hugely benefit much of the Congo, not least by decreasing mosquito populations. GMO should not be hastily undertaken, but when millions of children are dying from malaria, I think genetic modification of that one species sounds like a life-saver."

At the funeral, it turned out that the minister had been a friend of Sid's for a long time. He compared Uncle Sid to King Solomon, who could describe all kinds of plants like the cedar and the hyssop, and taught about animals, birds, reptiles and fish.

"Solomon was a wise man. He loved and studied nature. That was certainly true of Sid, who spent his life studying insects. It was his passion, not just a job. He had a deep respect for God's creation."

Patrick asked his Grandma Meg about this, because he hadn't heard her brother talk much about the things he believed. Meg sighed and thought for a moment.

"Your Great Uncle Sid had some ideas about Bible prophecies that I didn't agree with, Pat. But he loved God and nature and looked forward to meeting the one who made it all." She smiled. "That's a good way to be!"

On one of their final cleaning days at Sid's cabin, Patrick came across a drawer full of cut out bar codes. His father laughingly explained that Uncle Sid had always mistrusted bar codes, just as he did credit cards. It was all part of a "one world system" which would manipulate people around the globe.

Rachel didn't join in his mirth. She paused in the clean-up of Sid's office area.

"You know, Pete, there's talk of replacing our credit cards and passport ID with a microchip under our skin. Thousands of people in Sweden think it's a great idea. Is it possible Sid may have been right about some things? Imagine being tracked everywhere by a system that holds all your information!"

She changed the topic. "Patrick, Uncle Sid would want you to have this." Rachel had found the Jurassic Park amber which Patrick had given Sid for his birthday.

That evening Pat placed the amber replica with its prehistoric mosquito on his own dresser. Beside it was the photo showing himself and a delighted Uncle Sid. In lots of ways, Pat missed him.

Paciencia!

Back when Peter himself was a child, his parents Arthur and Meg Paynton rarely spoke Spanish at home unless it was for secrets from the children or, in times of frustration, to counsel their kids to have patience: "Paciencia!" This was never actually translated, so Peter and his sister Tabi garnered the sense of the word from the contexts and attitudes of their parents when they said it. If a bill came to more than Arthur had anticipated, he would sigh, smile grimly, fold his arms, shrug his shoulders and pronounce to Meg, "Paciencia!" If Tabi and Peter were really looking forward to a visit with relatives but something unexpected thwarted the plans, or Christmas parcels didn't arrive in time from England or the sports day at school was rained out, their mother, seeing their downcast faces, would smile gently, give them a hug and tell them, "Paciencia!" That was the final word, indicating that there was nothing they could do to change circumstances, closing that unhappy chapter and moving on with life. Inwardly the children struggled, but complaints were fruitless and they realized that even parents could not alter those situations.

Decades later, as teens or young adults, for similar frustrating situations they heard another word used by Canadian friends: "Whatever!" But this resignation to circumstances—or to ***whatever*** someone else had decided—was usually petulant, pretending that something didn't matter when it clearly did.

"Paciencia!", on the other hand, acknowledged the frustrations as real. Early in childhood Pete and Tabi learned that patience was one of the Biblical "fruits of the Spirit", and fitted with the words of the Apostle Paul: "All things work together for good for those who love God". In that context, patience is a product of believing that God is in control, no matter what obstacles we may encounter, and that we can expect God's provision if we just hold on. All that in one word!

Naturally, that stayed with Peter through the years of challenges and setbacks. He didn't lose his faith. On more than one occasion he found he was saying that word aloud to remind himself. And distressing circumstances and news can so easily catch us unprepared.

Like a few summers back when the Federal government unexpectedly refused student work grants to any organization which supported Pro Life. Pete's parents had stepped up to the plate and provided the missing funds for their church to hire two students during the summer university break. One of the students was their grandson Patrick, but they would have done it anyway. On the Sunday afternoon after they heard about the problem, Meg had told Arthur that it was high time to sell the rowboat parked in their driveway. What was the point, she said, in sanding and varnishing a boat you never put in the water? Pete thought that a bit harsh. It had been part of Arthur's dream in moving to the Comox Valley to finally buy a Whitehall sculling rowboat. He loved the look of lapstrake hulls and the practicality of fibreglass, but leapt at the chance, when it came, to buy his neighbour's wooden equivalent, even though the seat was fixed and the little boat required annual maintenance. The clinchers in the deal had been the trailer thrown in as well as his neighbour's obvious love for what had been built in his garage over several years. But Meg wasn't keen to go out on the water unless they were fishing, so any trip for rowing was by himself and the truth was, Arthur hadn't taken the boat down to the wharf in over two years. To Peter's great surprise, his father didn't protest. He sold the craft almost overnight and gave 80% of the money to the church for summer student salaries. There had been about a thousand dollars left over with which Arthur bought himself a second hand electric bike. He said it was exactly what he wanted.

More recently, there had been the fallout from "Capling vs. Scott". Waves of disbelief rolled across Canada when the Supreme Court upheld Ontario's decision in the court case, and editorials condemning the decision were immediate. How could any court rule in favour of terminating the life of a healthy toddler? But there it was, presented as an extension of the legal arguments in numerous abortion cases. If the happiness of a pregnant woman determined whether or not to carry a fetus to the moment of birth, why shouldn't that same criterion be the final word in whether or not a woman continued to look after a young child after it was born, or terminated it? The logic was horrifying, yet the defense for Capling had won despite protests of her partner, Scott. He had argued for custody of the child, but the court had agreed that the mother's rights prevailed. She had carried the fetus in her womb for 9 months, breast fed and cared for the baby for a year, and it was therefore her child to do with as she wished. If she did not want to allow her partner to bring up the child, or if she did not want to give it up for adoption, that was her prerogative. The accommodating physician had been exonerated.

Unbelievably, the editorials gradually softened in their presentation of the decision. The writers reflected that the case was a "one-off", not typical because of . . . well, any number of reasons. And "why should Ms. Capling be saddled with the responsibilities of child-raising when her heart lay in continuing her university studies?"

Just a few weeks later, there were similar cases—2 in Ontario and 3 in Quebec. Two of the cases involved toddlers older than the Capling baby, so there were court challenges. Since provincial childcare was funded for children aged 2 to 4, and pre-school was available after that, the courts determined that the Capling decision would not apply to children over the age of 2.

With this limitation and precedents in place, the furor quieted down. In all the provinces similar cases were occurring, but without publicity. Letters to the Editor and editorials about the issue rarely appeared, probably because people don't want to hear the same arguments repeated. It's boring.

Fortunately, within the church there was a consensus of opinion. It was one thing to abort a fetus which had no name and so perhaps was not really human; it was quite another to hear the cry of a newborn child, witness its growing personhood, then deny its right to life. Several of the larger churches set up "Young Mother Care Groups", hoping to assist any who might be desperate. This lasted only a few months before the federal government took away the tax exemption of any church seeking to influence the decisions of women.

Pete and Rachel, his wife, were part of the same church community as his parents and remembered how Arthur and Meg had bailed out the church when the government had turned down church applications for student work grants. Pete and others met to discuss the current situation, deciding to begin a "Young Mother Care Group", foregoing the tax exemption status. Momentarily, they felt relieved to have resolved this issue. Shortly, however, the provincial Health Minister announced that every Care Group still in operation must have a government appointed representative of Women's Rights, someone who would ensure that the option of terminating unwanted children be explained to young mothers. This person's salary would be the responsibility of the Care Group.

The Payntons and their whole group were aghast, seeing their tax exemption evaporate, and then a salary imposed. Could they afford it? More important, what was the point in having a Care

Group if some uninvited guest was going to constantly undermine it?

The situation was shared with leaders of the church denomination based in Toronto and a solution was proposed. The Moderator and others said the church as a whole needed to really examine the Bible to see whether perhaps the Capling decision might be correct. From time to time, they said, theological positions needed to be revised to accommodate a cultural shift and new understandings. How could Christians expect the Bible to have an answer to every question? DM (Discontinuing Motherhood) was not specifically referred to in Scripture, so it was a new, difficult and complex issue for the church. In the present case, people needed to get past those isolated Bible texts which seem to value even very young children. Such texts may be unhelpful in the church's desire to be seen as relevant and to move forward. Since Jesus said, "I have come that they may have life, and have it to the full", would he not be in favour of a life free from unpleasant responsibilities? They needed to appoint a study committee to articulate a new position. Ms. Capling and those like her were not violent people. On the contrary, they were good Canadian citizens.

In short order, the Synod appointed a committee to provide pastoral advice on the Capling ruling. The Committee sought out and interviewed young women considering DM or what was also called "the Capling option". After numerous meetings with other denominational groups, a Synod Report on Maternal Rights was published, and hailed as "wonderfully progressive" with the "groundbreaking conclusion" that the Canadian Supreme Court had been right all along. The church simply needed to be in sync with societal change.

When Peter recounted to his father this ecclesiastical "about-face", and how disillusioned he and Rachel felt about the church leadership, Arthur nodded, and sighed deeply. "Y bueno... He shrugged. "Paciencia!"

"Dad!" Peter protested, "We might not be able to persuade people who don't believe. But now this is inside the church itself where we claim to hold a different standard. Surely we should resist this thinking within the church."

Arthur smiled grimly. "If you think you can make a difference there, Pete, then you'd better do it." There was resignation in his tone, and Peter understood why. His father was in his 80s, tired, his fighting days behind him.

What was harder to understand was the quick resignation by people Peter's own age, some who told him that they didn't want to debate what had already been decided by the church council. "Let's get on with more important issues," said one friend. That was hard to swallow. What could be more important than valuing and protecting life itself?

The same friend, Warren, met Peter a few weeks later for their monthly Saturday brunch at Locals Restaurant in the Old House. Evidently the man was agitated about something and as they sat with coffee, awaiting their food orders, he began immediately. "There's a young MP who's put forward a bill. They're calling it "Responsible Retirement". The idea is that a reasonable life-span should not exceed 80, that people older than that are using up valuable resources while contributing nothing to the economy, that they should relinquish life voluntarily or be relieved of it by force, if necessary, for the good of others!"

"That idea is probably dead in the water," replied Peter. "Just think of the numbers of older MPs and senators. They won't pass it."

"That's just it!" continued Warren, very agitated. "Two years ago the obligatory retirement age for MPs and senators was set at 60. For the first time in Canadian history, we have a Senate with no one over that age. And half of the MPs this year are under the age of 45. There's no sympathy for older people. Believe it or not, there's cross party support for this bill and it's already passed first reading. "

"Ah, don't worry about it," countered Peter. "Canadians won't go for that plan."

"They won't have a choice!" said his friend. "CPP and OAP will be discontinued at age 80. Government plans to freeze private plans. Plus, there's an incentive package for cooperation, where next-of-kin receive 3 months of CPP payments or 50% of any assets, whichever is greater. And the penalty for ***not*** cooperating is that your family will lose 80% of your assets. It's a cash grab!"

This poured out of his friend and certainly sounded alarming. If this Machiavellian scheme were true, there was no time to be lost. Secretly Peter determined to research the facts that night on the Internet, then compose letters to MPs and committees he thought he might influence. There might already be an online petition he could sign. But for the moment . . .

Suppressing a smile, he reflected ruefully that protecting life certainly mattered to this man when it touched him personally; Warren was older and had recently celebrated a 75th birthday.

So Peter shrugged and replied casually in Spanish, "Paciencia!"

"What does ***that*** mean?" asked Warren.

"Oh," said Pete flippantly and only partly honest, "In this context, it's something like '***whatever***'. You know, ***whatever*** Parliament decides is just fine. After all, they know what's best, don't they?"

Feeling a little vindictive, he added Warren's own words, "Let's get on with more important issues."

Academic

When Patrick Paynton graduated, he eagerly enrolled in his first year at the University of Victoria, three hours south of the Comox Valley. He was excited to be entering the world of enlightenment, reason and research. On a more mundane level, entering the academic world was an opportunity to live away from home, to be independent. Patrick's mother smiled through the August afternoon of watching him pack up, but wept silently when his old Mazda pulled out of the driveway. Her mother-in-law, Meg, was there for the goodbyes. She, too, was wiping away tears.

Pat had managed to get a room in the dorms with one roommate, Claude Villiers from Belgium. He was a young man sent abroad to learn English for the family business, but he was not particularly motivated to do anything apart from hang out in the Mystic Market eating fish and chips or curried noodles. Claude was often out till all hours, so their lives were quite separate. Except when it came to assignments. It was Claude's lucky break that his roommate was willing to correct the grammar of many of the papers Claude submitted for marking.

For Pat, two things loomed large. He had begun courses in Anthropology, the door for his planned career in classical Archaeology. Just as important, he was meeting like-minded students in Varsity Christian Fellowship, students keen to live out their faith within their academic disciplines. He loved the challenge of discussions, debates, Tuesday noon Bible studies. Before long he was invited to join the leadership team for planning events, club meetings, speakers.

The VCF treasurer, Sophia Pappas, was a second year Philosophy undergrad. She was enthralled with one small assigned text, the "Meditations" of Roman Emperor Marcus Aurelius. "Listen to this!" she exclaimed before their executive meeting began, then regaled Pat and the others with one of the wise sayings of the Emperor:

"Think constantly, both as a Roman and as a man, to do the task before you with perfect and simple dignity, and with kindness, freedom, and justice."

"Sounds impressive," admitted Pat, "but that emperor also condoned the persecution and execution of Christians."

"How do you know that?" asked Sophia, taken aback.

"It's in the early Church History by Eusebius, the Bishop of Caesarea," replied Pat. "It's a book I'm hoping to finish before next summer."

Sophia and Pat had long conversations and she became a close friend.

They worked together on many projects, painting posters for special events in the SUB, and surreptitiously unrolling the 20 foot long posters out second story windows of the McPherson Library, Pat awkwardly taping the top to the building wall while Sophia secured it at ground level.

She was genuinely interested in Pat's discipline, Archaeology. He was busy researching previous attempts to find Moses' crossing of the Red Sea. "Just imagine if we could uncover some of the Egyptian chariots stuck in the mud where they pursued the Israelites! There's a good chance the mud would have preserved the metal." To his disappointment, in North American universities the focus was on New World archaeology, with digs, papers, projects concentrating on prehistory of the indigenous peoples.

Anthropology majors had to wade through courses in social and cultural anthropology, reading and writing about kinship systems. This was a far cry from Pat's dream of underwater archaeology in the Mediterranean. Still, he understood that his career goal involved jumping hoops and he persevered. In his spare time he continued his own research into likely points for Moses' crossing of the Red Sea, and investigated being a student volunteer for ongoing summer excavation of Tel Gezer in Israel.

Two Saturdays a month Sophia went to a low cost housing complex where she had been building friendships with families. Pat appreciated this practical application of her faith, and accompanied her on occasion. Wanting to give a wilderness adventure to the inner-city kids, he arranged with some of the families that he would take their children on a hike in Mount Doug Park. He and Sophia squeezed six hyper pre-teens into the back of Pat's Mazda and drove to the wilderness park for a hike to a cave hidden in the bush. The exuberance of the group and Pat's clowning around distracted Sophia from her claustrophobic reaction to the narrow cave entrance. Thankfully, they made it back without an incident, returning the kids to their families.

Patrick's folks, Pete and Rachel, tried to have one FaceTime call a week to hear about university life, but there were weeks which went by without any call. His grandparents heard his news second hand from Rachel. They all anticipated eagerly Pat's return to the Comox Valley for Christmas Break. The evening of December 21st was memorable! There was the dinner itself. Rachel had prepared his favourite: roast beef, Yorkshire pudding, mashed potatoes, gravy made with the drippings, green bean casserole topped with crispy onion rings. Over the leisurely meal, Pat answered their questions about dorm life and classes. He told them about his original research paper on dendrochronology of the Pacific Northwest—creating a tree ring record for dating wooden objects of the past 1000 years on the south B.C. coast.

Grandpa Arthur was enthusiastic. "That sounds intriguing, Patrick. I wish I could have learned about that when I studied history."

Patrick laughed. "Actually, Papa, I didn't realize that anything predating the explorers is technically '***pre***-historic', even if it's only 500 years old, because there's no written history to interpret what you find. It's not like Europe or Asia, where written history goes back thousands of years. And what you find is pretty basic stuff because the Stone Age in North America lasted right up until recently. A simple petroglyph here could have been carved at the same time as William the Conqueror was building the Tower of London. I can see that North American archaeology is necessary to discover more about indigenous cultures, but it's not what I want to spend my life doing."

Grandma Meg slipped away from the table and reappeared from the kitchen with hot apple strudel and ice cream. She cut the strudel, putting pieces on dessert plates and passed these to her husband for dollops of ice cream. Pete was collecting the dinner plates and taking them to the kitchen.

"All right," said Meg, "now tell us about your friend Sophia. What does she think about all this?"

Her grandson laughed. "You know what she gave me, all wrapped up for Christmas? A special issue of American Anthropology West entitled, "Burial Techniques among the Mazarundi".

They all laughed and Pete said, "Sounds like a real page-turner! Obviously, Sophia's got a good sense of humour!"

"We bug each other about our chosen majors," said Patrick. "Yeah—we have fun. She's a good sport. When I had to collect tree ring data, she came to help drill the trees with a Swedish increment borer. And I do respect what ***she's*** studying. Ultimately, we should ***all*** be philosophers; we should all be 'lovers of wisdom', of understanding". You know, if I get my doctorate in Anthropology, it'll be a PhD, a doctorate in philosophy, because I'll be contributing new research to one aspect of knowledge. That's the idea anyway. "

There were other great conversations—around meals, on family walks by the river or out at the Spit. Christmas Day itself was special for Patrick—his first 'coming home' Christmas after months away. When the few days of his holiday were over and his Mazda drove south again, his parents and grandparents sat around the quieter living room and marveled at how sophisticated and intellectual Pat had become, how capably he expressed his thoughts. University studies obviously suited him.

On the drive back down Island to UVIC, Patrick listened to a CD he had been given, a lecture on the Christian mottos of many universities. The lecture was 45 minutes long, so he had ample time to play it twice, trying to retain as many details as possible. University mottos are almost always in Latin. When translated into English, it becomes clear that many look to God as the source of light and truth. Oxford's Latin motto is "The Lord is my light", from Psalm 27. Glasgow has "The way, the truth, the life." The University of Freiburg has Christ's words, "The truth will set you free", the same motto adopted by Johns Hopkins University. Harvard's motto in Latin, dating to 1692, translates as "Truth for Christ and the Church", although secularization has reduced this to "Veritas" (Truth). Princeton's motto: "Under the protection of God, she flourishes." Columbia: "In thy light shall we see light." In Canada, the University of Alberta takes its motto from Paul's letter to the Philippians: "Whatsoever things are true".

For many of the university founders, apparently, all truth was seen as God's truth, and Christian faith was a springboard for inquiry. It was invigorating, exciting stuff to listen to! Even the University of Victoria got a mention. Patrick was surprised to learn that above the crest for UVIC, written in Hebrew, is "Let there be light" from Genesis 1.

Varsity Christian Fellowship was up and running again and Pat wondered about hosting a symposium on "Truth and Objectivity". Can something be true even if you can't establish it via the scientific method? Is truth the same as objectivity? What did Jesus mean when he said, "I am the truth"? How about inviting some Christian profs from various departments to discuss the differences between truth and objectivity?

Before suggesting the symposium to the VCF executive, Pat decided to run it past Dr. Whyting, his prof for Anthro 100. Patrick had been pleasantly surprised to run into him one Sunday in a local Anglican Church where his prof was reading the Bible from the pulpit. It turned out that Dr. Whyting was an occasional lay reader! How would Dr. Whyting view his own Christian faith in relation to his academic career? Pat arranged a meeting in the man's office, explained his idea for the symposium, and invited the professor to consider participation.

To his dismay, Dr. Whyting took offense, declaring emphatically, "I will NOT use my position as a platform for proselytizing!" Wow! Patrick could hardly believe it. He picked up his books and left quietly. The prof had responded as if he had been asked to do something dishonest! Really? Was religious truth to be put in a compartment separate from the rest of life? As he walked back to the dorms, he struggled with what had just happened. It was disheartening. If a prof in his own department wouldn't consider participating, how could Pat expect other students to approach their professors?

Over coffee with Sophia, Patrick explained to her what had happened with Dr. Whyting. She was aghast and words poured out of her in a torrent.

"You must have felt awful! You weren't in any way asking him to compromise his position as a prof. You just wanted others to see that among the profs we look up to, there are Christians, people who think, who haven't thrown away their brains. Some people think you have to leave your faith at the door when you enter academic studies."

It was quite a speech. Pat felt relieved that she understood and shared his dismay.

"What do you think, Soph? Should I still suggest the symposium to the executive? We know strong Christian profs on campus, people who might still like the idea, and agree to participate."

Sophia smiled warmly at him.

"I love your seriousness, Pat. Actually, I . . . " There was a long pause. "I like the idea of contrasting truth and objectivity, of showing that they aren't the same."

"But . . . ?" He waited for the conclusion.

"Would a symposium on truth and objectivity change anybody's mind? It might be better 'in house', maybe a good discussion for the spring camp on Thetis Island."

Pat sighed heavily. Sophia could tell he felt defeated.

"Hey, Pat. If we were going ahead with the symposium, you know we'd spend at least a day getting everything ready. Why not spend that day instead with the kids from the housing complex? I've heard of a great trail out in East Sooke at Aylard Farm. There's even a petroglyph for you to explain to them. Building those relationships might be a lot more meaningful than making a point which doesn't change anyone. And I'd sure look forward to a day like that—with you."

It was a sweet moment and he smiled back, taking her hand in his.

"Okay, Soph. Maybe winning that point about truth and objectivity would just be . . . academic."

Golden Boy

Peter Paynton warms his hands around a cup of coffee and sits staring out at falling snow. Unbelievably, he is retired now, like his own father, Arthur. He is thankful not to have to drive in to school. But he is thankful also for the strange ways in which blessings have come even through hard times. He glances at an old teacup on his library shelf and remembers Frank.

Frank Salloway was one of the most difficult students in the years Peter taught elementary classes. Frank was a good-looking athletic boy whose initial politeness did not betray his underlying mean streak. The meanness was reported to Peter by his principal in the first week of that grade 4/5 split, when it turned out that Frank had cornered a timid plump boy on his homeward route, then pushed him to the ground and forced dog poop into his mouth. Frank kept his own mouth firmly shut when taken to the principal's office the next day and asked about the incident. He smiled insolently, but refused to talk. Detention time solved nothing. Roger, the victim, next day reported his bike tires slashed. All the staff suspected Frank, but couldn't prove it.

If 'Mr. Paynton' took the class to the gym for P.E., before much time had elapsed, Frank had climbed one of the ropes and was walking along ceiling beams, daring others to do the same. In class it often happened that when Peter turned to talk to his students after writing on the board, someone would be crying or nursing a punched shoulder, while Frank smiled annoyingly from his desk nearby.

But he was good in Math, and Peter made a point of complimenting him for it in front of the class. When they made stick puppets using bamboo rods, chunks of foam for heads and scraps of cloth, Frank created an amazing monster then proceeded to chase other puppets around the room. Seeing that most were enjoying the game, Pete laughed along with them, then halted the chase and had Frank hold up his creation. Peter pointed out how Frank had cleverly glued on googly eyes and used a mop for hair. Frank got to pick two other students to work on a puppet show and present it to the class.

Somehow they made it through the year without more than one major incident each month. On the final day in June, when several students gave their teacher cards and thank you gifts, to Peter's surprise, Frank solemnly placed on the teacher desk a cracked and stained teacup and saucer, then stood awkwardly waiting for a response. Although not wrapped, the cup was clearly meant as a gift. Other students had formed a line, eager for Mr. Paynton to open their gifts, but they would have to wait. Peter picked up the cup and examined it appreciatively, then looked back at Frank just as solemnly and thanked him for his thoughtfulness. In gold lettering on the cup were the words "Golden Boy". Inwardly Pete smiled at the irony. From Frank, his "Golden Boy" of the year! But that teacup represented a hard-won relationship and for many years it sat on a bookshelf in his study.

Patrick, the "Golden Boy" from the Paynton household, is far from the family home in Comox. He has another year to complete his B.A. at the University of Victoria. His parents, both retired, specially look forward to occasional weekends and summer months when their son returns from his dorm life at UVIC. In the days between visits, their house seems strangely quiet.

Peter Paynton and his son Patrick have long enjoyed vigorous debates about politics, faith, art and music. Like his father, Patrick thinks that deciding on the "right" position about any topic and expressing it goes a long way toward solving problems. Peter generally defends traditional established views, while Patrick generally thinks those views must be wrong because they ***are*** traditional and they haven't succeeded in eliminating unhappiness. It's predictable, and Rachel despairs of having a meal time where nothing controversial is discussed.

A recent discussion about "tent cities" is typical. Peter maintains homeless people should be accommodated outside city limits, making sure that basic necessities are provided. Patrick counters that the mess downtown can't be avoided because homeless people need to have easy walking access to stores. Peter brings up the problem with transients moving to whichever city will tolerate and provide for them. Patrick retorts that store owners and homeowners shouldn't just think of their own comfort.

Rachel rarely gets in a word edgewise, but on this occasion she has read a related article in "West Coast Currents", so she breaks into the dinner duel.

"You know, there's a church down-Island which is doing something about homelessness. They've created a company for building plastic igloos on their own site. The igloo design and recycled plastic apparently makes construction way cheaper. It keeps out winter cold, easily reaching comfortable temperatures without more than a simple little heater. Already they have 12 of the igloos built and ready for occupants."

Peter is interested, but skeptical. "What's the church?"

"The Church of Enoch."

"I've never heard of it before." Pete is dubious. "Sounds like a cult to me."

"Yeah, it's a cult," confirms Patrick. "They bought the old Community Hall on Janetka Road and have started building little houses for church members around the baseball field. I guess the igloos will be on the soccer field just below. Their music sounds pretty cool, though."

"What's different about their music?" asks his mother.

"They use only musical instruments named in the Old Testament—Shofars, lyres, flutes and timbrels," Patrick answers. "The timbrel is like a tambourine. They sing, of course, but they don't use harmony, only melody. And their Bibles have to be the King James Version."

"Sounds like a cult, all right," pronounces his father. "No accountability to a larger denomination—just running off with their own interpretation of what it means to be a Christian."

Rachel is amazed that her son knows so much about the group. "How do you know all that?"

"Sophia has a friend whose father is the pastor in the Church of Enoch. Soph met her working at the Food Bank. Her friend always wears long skirts and never any make-up. Like I said," Patrick concludes, "It's a cult."

This is one of the few dinner debates which have included Rachel, and she is keen to continue.

"Still, if the Church of Enoch is doing something to help homeless people, maybe they deserve some respect. Maybe we could learn something from them, getting involved instead of just talking about problems." She looks meaningfully at her husband and her son.

Patrick glances at his phone and excuses himself. There's a text from Sophia, he explains, and he has to talk to her.

After their son leaves the room, Peter sits quietly thinking. "You're right, Rachel. It's the parable of the two sons. One of them says the wrong thing, but then he changes his mind, gets off his butt and helps his father. Maybe . . ." he sighs, "maybe ***he***'s the father's 'Golden Boy'. Maybe . . . I could help to put together some of those igloos."

Divining

Last summer Peter and Rachel Paynton bit the bullet and hired a landscaper to re-surface their front lawn. Pete had given up on his original plan of attacking one square meter a day, pulling weeds and re-seeding. It turned out that many of the weeds had roots going down to the other side of the planet. Peter and Rachel discussed the options. Perhaps they could call the weed patch a 'pasture' instead of a lawn; that might make the weeds legitimate, even necessary! Neither of them really believed in this solution, so with a sigh, the landscaper was brought in.

Re-surfacing that lawn meant stripping off the existing couch-grass, importing 30 yards of top-soil and levelling it before applying sod. "But this will all be useless," the landscaper told the Payntons, "if you don't have a way of watering the new lawn during the dry summer months. So, again with a sigh, installation of a watering system was included in the plan.

The landscaper maintained this would be easily connected to the main water line wherever it entered the house. To the Payntons' dismay, where the water line entered the house was impossible to find, even after a thorough search on hands and knees in the crawl space. A plumber discovered that the main water line came up through the cement floor beside their hot water tank where there was no easy way to connect to the new lawn watering system.

Consequently, they would have to find some access to the main line outside where it approached the house, somewhere underground.

Thus began a time-consuming search for the main line, which snaked underground from the water meter 100 yards away and reappeared through the cement floor beside the water tank. Municipal records mapped nothing beyond the water meter, which was at the bottom of a long driveway. Helpfully, their landscaper suggested they contact a friend of his who had very expensive water detection equipment. Peter had never heard of such equipment and was intrigued.

A call to this man, Bernie, resulted in a visit from him, but not with the expensive equipment. He stepped out of his pickup truck carrying two short foot-long wires of the kind used for clothes hangers. Each of the two wires was bent in an 'L' shape. Bernie explained that water witching had worked very well for him personally, and that he would not normally suggest this for his clients, but that it was worth a try since bringing the heavy equipment would be difficult and expensive.

Water witching? Peter tried not to grin. He was skeptical, but remembered that his own father Arthur had hired a man to water-witch for a well site. "If it works," he said doubtfully, "it has nothing to do with spirits. Why would it work?"

"It works, all right," Bernie assured him, "and I think I know why, although no one has proved it. About two hundred years ago there was an Italian doctor named Luigi Galvani who discovered something similar when he was examining a dissected frog. The dead frog was hanging from a metal hook when Galvani noticed the frog kick."

Peter was incredulous. "What's the connection with water witching?"

Bernie explained. "It turns out that the frog's body was perfect for sensing electricity. So…who knows? Maybe there is some magnetism or electricity which would explain why water witching works. Would you like me to witch your underground pipe?"

Peter had not quite followed the reasoning. "How much do you charge for this?" he asked.

"Normally I would only do this for myself and for friends," said Bernie. "My usual business is excavation of surface wells. If I do this for you, I guess you could pay me one hour at my usual rate: $90 an hour, one hour minimum. It would cost a lot more if I use my heavy gear," he added.

Peter hesitated. Ninety dollars for a hillbilly solution? Still, if it worked . . . "I'll think about it and phone you later this evening."

Bernie shrugged. "It's your call. Check out Galvani's frog on the internet."

After his visitor had driven away, Pete went straight to his computer to verify the strange story. Articles about Luigi Galvani were easy to find and Peter read several, poring over the diagrams and line drawings.

His son Patrick was home for a couple of days from university MA studies and Peter asked what he knew of the Italian physician and professor Galvani. Pat was surprised his father hadn't heard of the frog incident, and enthusiastically filled him in.

"Galvani taught anatomy. He dissected frogs because they were easy to get and provided a simple way to examine muscles and nerves. One day he hung a dead frog on an iron railing beside their house and he was startled to see the dead frog kick. Galvani thought he was seeing some sort of animal electricity—maybe like an electric eel."

Rachel came into the study to find out how the search for water had gone. Her husband described the odd visit and Bernie's suggestion to try water witching. "He thinks it works like Galvani and the frog," said Pete, and repeated what Pat had just told him.

"You're pulling my leg!" quipped Rachel. When Patrick groaned, she said, "Okay, okay. I'm interested. What else do you know?"

Patrick glanced at the article which his father had up on the computer screen, and remembered more of the story.

"Another Italian, Alessandro Volta, disagreed with Galvani, saying that the electricity was produced by the iron railing and the copper hook used to hang the dead frog." Patrick digressed for a moment. "Volta was a pretty impressive scientist himself, studying the effects of electricity on taste and touch. He discovered that when he placed a coin on top of his tongue and a coin of a different metal underneath his tongue, that a wire connecting the two coins carried an electric current, causing the coins to taste salty."

"That's interesting," said Rachel. "So if I put a nickel under my tongue and a loonie on top of it, it'll taste salty."

"If you link the two coins with a wire—yes. At least, that's what Volta found," said Patrick. "Anyway," he continued, "to prove that Galvani's frog was reacting to electricity between the two metals, Volta created a simple battery with alternating layers of zinc, wet cardboard, silver, finally linking the top and bottom with a wire to create a flow of electricity."

Rachel broke in, "So Galvani was wrong and Volta got credit for the battery?"

Now Patrick remembered more of the story from his Biology 12 class.

"Actually, Galvani was correct in many of his ideas about bioelectricity, even though he was wrong about why the frog kicked. Volta was right about how the metals worked, but he respected Galvani and called the electricity 'Galvanism.'"

Peter read out what he had found online. "Luigi Galvani still maintained that there was electricity present in the frog's body without the metals. But rather than argue with Volta, he went on with his work as a doctor, apparently treating poor people whether or not they could pay his fees. An amazing man, eh?"

Rachel was thoughtful. "It seems each of them was generous—cutting the other some slack."

Continuing to read silently, Peter suddenly burst into laughter.

"Ha! Galvani actually developed a device to detect electricity: the Frog Galvanoscope!"

They all laughed. Peter chortled as he read:

"A frog's hind leg including the big sciatic nerve is cut from the body of a recently killed frog . . . . The leg is skinned and placed in a glass tube with just the nerve available for connecting wires. Even a tiny electric current makes the leg twitch--and this instrument can work for almost 2 days before a fresh leg is needed. The frog leg was much more sensitive to an electric current than other instruments then available."

Rachel wanted to get back to her emails, but threw back a final comment as she left the room. "Can't you just see it—an electrical inspector walking around with a frog leg in a test tube!"

Patrick grinned and left to do more of his MA research.

Well, Bernie had told the truth about Galvani's frog; perhaps there really was something to water witching. Peter phoned Bernie and confirmed that he would like to try it. He also phoned his father Arthur to let him know about the water divining demonstration taking place the next day. "How about you and Mum bring some lawn chairs to watch the show? Stay for the day. We'll have dinner together."

Chairs were set up next morning at 9:30 facing the field of action. Arthur, Meg, Rachel and Peter shared a thermos of coffee as they awaited the event. Unfortunately, Patrick would have to miss out; he had returned to UVIC for a few days. Around 10 a white pickup truck pulled in and parked in the driveway. A door slammed and Bernie walked over with his 'L' shaped wires. Everyone was introduced then Pete asked, "Before you begin, can you explain to us how Galvani's discovery connects with water divining?"

"Okay," the water detector told his audience of four. "About 20 years after Galvani's frog, there was another totally unrelated discovery. Somebody noticed that the needle on a compass jumped around whenever it came close to a magnet. Years later, people discovered that a magnetic field can be created by an electric current. So that meant that you might locate underground wires just by watching your compass needle as you walk around a property. When the needle jumps, the wires or something magnetic is close by. Pretty cool, huh? So," he added proudly, "This is my idea. ***I*** think it might be possible for water flowing in a pipe to act like a magnet—enough to pull these wires to line up with the water pipe underground."

Bernie slipped the small end of each wire into a short copper pipe which he held in his fists, then positioned the two long ends loosely parallel to each other and facing ahead, like pistols ready to fire. He explained that the loose position in the pipes would allow the wires to move without human influence. Arthur got up from his lawn chair and stood close by where he could better see the wires move.

Having ascertained from the Payntons where they imagined the line to approach the house under the lawn, Bernie walked slowly across the area like some marshal out of the Old West, both guns drawn and stealthily closing in on an outlaw. As he edged across the lawn, he told them, "Holding these wires steady is really exhausting."

When he arrived at the suspected location, the two wires swung inward, toward each other and remained in a line between his two fists. This seemed promising. He took a spray can from one of his pockets and sprayed a blue X on the grass. Several more passes established a line of Xs, all leading from the driveway to the closest corner of the house. Strange, thought Peter, he hadn't seen a pipe in that part of the crawl space.

Whatever the explanation, now he knew where to dig. He was delighted and paid Bernie for his time and expertise. Arthur and Meg stayed for dinner as planned and told about witching their well the year Peter had been in grade three. And, of course, that led to all sorts of memories.

Digging the lawn next day proved incredibly difficult. Like other properties on the hillside, a thin veneer of lawn soil covered shale and clay. With a mattock and shovel, Pete slaved away that day and the next, producing a trench reminiscent of WWI. He hadn't timed this well since his son Pat wasn't available to help. There was no sign of any water line, even though he had gone down 4 to 5 feet in a trench stretching across the line of Xs. Tarps on the lawn now had piles of shale and sod. It has to be here, reasoned Peter, and extended his trench in both directions. As his father would say, "Not a sausage!"

Exhausted from his day's work, that evening he searched until he found a phone number for the previous owner. Fortunately, the former owner answered the phone. "No," she said after Peter had explained, "You won't find any water line under the lawn. The pipe goes up the driveway directly under the road all the way to the house."

Peter thanked her profusely. He felt relieved and irritated at the same time. All that ditch digging for nothing! Too bad he'd already paid for the water witching. The more he thought about it, the more certain he was that it had all been a scam. Bernie must've been laughing all the way to the bank! Well, he thought, there's one man I'll never see again!

The next day he hired a backhoe to unearth the water line, which was immediately located 3 feet down under one of the road ruts. Water was shut off and the landscaper inserted a water access "T" for the new sprinkler system. Peter, meanwhile, slogged away, shoveling back into the lawn trenches all of the shale and clay he had removed. Thankfully Patrick had driven home again for the weekend and was willing to help fill in holes.

To Pete's immense surprise, who should show up two days later but Bernie, the charlatan who had caused all the hassle! Struggling to hold back his anger, Peter walked up to the truck. Bernie was oblivious to Peter's bristling manner and asked eagerly, "So, did you find the line where I painted the Xs?"

Pete guffawed. "Not quite!" Walking him around the area, Peter described his own digging and the eventual pipe location under the driveway. He pointed out where the lawn trenches were now filled in and told about all the shale he had had to dig through.

"You wouldn't believe the hours that took!" he said, grimacing.

Bernie's face paled and he looked sick. "Honestly, I don't know why that didn't work. I'm sorry you did all that and found nothing . . . . I'll give you back what you paid."

At that point the truth dawned on Peter. He realized grudgingly that Bernie really must have expected a different result. There was no other reason for him to have come back after being paid.

Something inside Peter felt pulled—you might say, like a compass needle passing over a magnetic field. He was "divining" something. He thought of how Galvani and Volta had treated each other despite their disagreements.

His thoughts were interrupted when Patrick walked out from the house, taking a break from his studies. He joined his father who introduced him to Bernie.

"Perhaps," Pete returned to the conversation, "your water witching was responding to the overhead electric wires. Who knows? It might have worked."

Bernie looked pained. "Maybe," he said weakly.

Peter hesitated. Surely, intention mattered.

"Keep the money," he said firmly, and smiled. "I'm glad you told me about Galvani and the frog."

It was meant to ease the burden of his visitor, but clearly Bernie was struggling to accept this resolution. He looked restless, still mulling over the unsatisfactory course of events. Patrick broke in on the silence.

"So you've really seen it work?"

"Oh, yes!" Bernie took this like a lifeline. "Many times! In fact . . . just wait here."

He strode to his truck, opened the door briefly, slammed it shut, then quickly rejoined father and son, holding the 'L' shaped wires. He slipped them into the copper pipes which he had also brought, and eagerly positioned them in Patrick's hands.

"Divining takes practice," he said seriously. "Your Dad knows what to do, or you can find it online. I'd like you to have them."

"But they're yours," Patrick protested.

Bernie smiled with relief. "It's the least I can do. I can make more."

For just a moment Peter felt cheated. He had wanted to be the generous one. Now it was reciprocal—like Galvani and Volta. Besides, the water pipe had been found. Even if water witching sometimes worked, what possible use was there now for those wires?

Peter took a deep breath and smiled back. "Thanks!" he said. "It'll be a challenge to hold them steady. I hope we can get it right."

Christmas at last

'Tis the Season

Advent was beginning. After years of collecting ornaments, there were far too many for one little Christmas tree. So with the big day only a few weeks away, Meg had the idea to decorate a little tree in the forest close by. Very particular, she selected only red bulbs from the boxes and set out enthusiastically along their favourite woodland trail. Arthur tagged along for security, but also came in handy for hanging the little red bulbs on higher branches. Meg was delighted by the result and phoned her walking buddy Josie to tell her about the secret tree. Just a few days later, Meg and Arthur were again walking the trail and noticed other ornaments had joined their own—as many bulbs now of other colours and shapes, plus an ornate tinsel angel attached to the very top! Yes, Josie confirmed, she had added to the tree and now had left a gift under it for the Payntons. Meg retrieved the present, which included home-spiked eggnog with a card, then reciprocated with her own gift to Josie and Bill—a silhouette of the nativity scene, along with a box of shortbread cookies she had made. Josie phoned to thank Meg and to inform her that half the cookies had already been consumed.

The sharing of their forest tree was whimsical, and a joy to Meg.

Arthur's attention was elsewhere. The rodents had returned and found a way into the storage room. Three live traps were supplied with dabs of peanut butter and placed in strategic locations:

one by the furnace in the crawl space, one close to a crack in the garage door and the last in the basement storage room beside bags of dog food and bird seed.

It wasn't just mice. A bag of grass seed sitting on his outside work bench had been chewed. Rat droppings festooned the area where seed had been a nightly feast. Once discovered, the grass seed bag was repaired with duct tape and moved to safety inside. In its place Arthur put a rat trap, slathered generously with peanut butter. The next day he removed a dead rat from the trap and reset the trap. A week passed before the wily rats went for the bait. He bagged another limp rat body in a dog poop bag and dropped it in the garbage can. After that, no amount of peanut butter could coax remaining rats or mice, but each morning Arthur checked "the trap line."

Christmas Day arrived with socked-in west coast fog throughout the Comox Valley, but nothing spoiled the mood. Every aspect was enjoyed in slow motion: the arrival of Pete and Rachel with grandson Patrick home for the holidays, a video call from Tabi and her family, lighting of the Advent wreath candles, Patrick reading from the gospel of Luke, enjoying each other's surprise as presents were opened. Everyone got a chuckle from Meg's gift to her husband: a raccoon fur hat, a family heirloom from Great Grandpa Milne's time among the Dene up north, but now passed on, as she said in her card, "to the most recent trapper in the family". Then a change of menu—no turkey this year, but roast beef and Yorkshire pudding, ice cream and butter tarts, and of course catching up on each other's lives. What could be finer?

Meg examined the wreckage of torn paper afterward. She and Arthur cleaned up with a CD of The Messiah playing in the background.

"Let's not take anything down until Epiphany," she pleaded with Arthur. "Let's just enjoy this for the whole time."

Arthur sighed. "A lot of people take down their decorations before New Year's Day. They don't know anything about January 6th."

"So what?!" Meg replied, irritated. "What other people do doesn't have to apply in our own house!"

But she was taken aback when they passed their woodland tree on December 28th. Only their own red bulbs remained; everything else had been removed. Meg phoned Josie, inquired about her Christmas, and then mentioned her sadness over the decorations now taken from the forest tree.

Josie was startled. No, she said, she hadn't removed anything from the tree.

Talking it over with Arthur that evening, Meg wondered who might have removed Josie's ornaments. It had to be someone who knew which bulbs had been on the tree originally, because those had been left. Why would someone take only those bulbs which belonged to Josie? It was distressing, and Meg suddenly thought of Josie's neighbour who had helped himself to some of Josie's cucumber garden, then smirked about it when he told her later. That was the odd man who seemed to leer at Meg when he walked past her with his growling Pekinese. He was an unpredictable character, a middle-aged recluse who used the same forest trails—one reason Arthur liked to accompany her when she took the trail to Josie's house. In fact, that man had even scowled at Arthur wearing his raccoon hat on their walk the other day, and muttered something about the fur trade as they passed.

After Arthur heard about the mysterious theft, he and Meg went together to collect their own Christmas ornaments. Sure enough, all of the red bulbs remained. As they picked the final ornaments off the little tree and slipped them into Meg's shopping bag, Arthur noticed one ornament lying on the ground. Whoever had taken all the other bulbs must have dropped the special tinsel angel, which was lying underneath the tree. They took it home with them.

When Josie came over later that week, Meg gave her a plastic bag with the angel inside. "At least you got back one thing," she said, "even if all your bulbs are gone."

Josie was pleased and surprised. "Thanks! Actually, this is the only ornament I put on the tree. I thought all the bulbs were yours."

This revelation changed the whole picture! So whoever had removed the other bulbs was most likely the person who had put them on! And that person had considerately left the angel and Meg's red bulbs. Instead of revealing evil in the neighbourhood, what had happened actually showed good will from someone Meg didn't even know. She felt chastened. Could it even be . . .? But that was probably going too far. No, despite the "Boo Radley" surprise heroes in fiction, it probably wasn't Josie's weird neighbour. Meg would still want Arthur with her on the forest walks.

But it did make her think about how easily one can come to the wrong conclusion.

When she explained the whole thing to Arthur that evening, he laughed.

"But seriously, Art," she said," I think that man was by himself for Christmas. There's still a tin of shortbread. I'll box some up and we can drop it at his house next time I visit Josie." She added, a little anxiously, "You'll come, won't you?"

"I wouldn't miss it!" said Arthur with a grin. "Do you think I should leave my Davy Crockett hat at home?"

Mosslawns.com

"Peace on earth, goodwill to all." Every Christmas reminds us of this declaration by the angels. Christmas speaks of peace, the birth of the Prince of Peace. At Christmas time, even the secular world makes an effort to work at peace and goodwill. On Christmas Day 1914, for several hours German and English soldiers put down their guns, sang carols and crawled out of their trenches to shake hands and play soccer together. Because of Christmas Day, they acted like . . . well, like ***neighbours.***

Some neighbours of the Sheldons can hardly wait to celebrate the Christmas season. Across the street from their home lives Mike, a neighbor who sets up his Christmas lawn display on Remembrance Day. Yup—that's right! Remembrance Day! On the day the Sheldons come home from the cenotaph wearing poppies, they are greeted by the sight of giant candy canes, Santa and, outlined in lights, a sleigh pulled by a strangely shaped creature which does not so much resemble Rudolph, as it does a cross between a kangaroo and a rabbit. Emma Sheldon refers to it as "the Christmas Bunny".

Now, it's not just the crassness of this scenario which bugs them; it's the fact that Mike's eagerness to begin every holiday early sets the trend for the neighborhood. For example, scarcely had school begun this September than Mike set up the approach to his house for Hallowe'en: an enormous spider web, a row of angry grimacing pumpkins—and an eerie recorded werewolf howl! Within hours, it seemed, pumpkins appeared on other people's porches.

So when Jerry Sheldon saw the Christmas Bunny this Remembrance Day, he thought he might walk across, knock on Mike's door and offer to sell him Valentine's chocolates. You know—rub it in a little about celebrating events at the wrong time of year. Yes, I know—you're thinking this attitude doesn't fit with "good will to all".

But it was neighbourhood trends which led to Emma buying Jerry a lawnmower last Christmas. I mean—*a lawnmower??* Think about it! You tear off the Christmas wrap to discover . . . a Honda GCV which you *might* begin to use five months later! Jerry tried to sound enthusiastic and thankful, but the box went out to his garage and the mower manual stayed in its plastic wrap until May.

In the Sheldons' suburban neighborhood, as soon as warm weather threatens, the lawns of their neighbours are immaculate—well-groomed, free of weeds and moss, and impressively green. Ten years ago, when they first moved to Murrayville, Jerry was delighted by the beautiful landscapes until it was brought home to him that he was expected to keep their lawn in the same condition. One neighbor in particular made that clear. John, across the road, said that he and others had spent a fortune to free their lawns of weeds, that the seeds from the Sheldons' weeds might blow across the road and contaminate his grass, that Jerry should use weed-killer the same as everybody else. Jerry was annoyed that a neighbour thought he had the right to say what the Sheldons could do on their own turf, but the point was made.

Emma and Jerry have never felt comfortable with chemical weed-killers—the thought of animals walking across a treated lawn then licking their paws, or worms recoiling from chemical solutions, or birds eating the worms and spreading poison through the food chain. How much of this would actually occur remains doubtful, but misgivings about chemicals persist. So Jerry spent hours on his knees in the yard, manually pulling up buttercups. He also researched natural treatments for lawn weeds, ordered the products online, and applied them hopefully. Not much changed. The telltale clover, dandelions, buttercups showed up anyway. As someone has wisely observed, if at first you don't succeed, destroy all evidence that you tried in the first place! That's why mowing helps; from a distance, mown weeds look pretty similar to a well-groomed lawn.

But mowing that corner lot takes a lot of time, and Jerry put off bringing out his Christmas Honda GCV mower for the first spring mowing until the tidy surrounding lawns made his overgrown grass and weeds stand out. There are lots of things he'd rather do than mow the lawn and he had just recently been offered an especially fine alternative. A friend going away on a cruise holiday had offered to loan Jerry for a whole month his sporty green Miata. A spin down along the beach in a sports car sure beats mowing a lawn!

Unfortunately, the Miata had not yet been delivered, so reluctantly, on a sunny spring afternoon he hauled out the mower and started it up. John was out sitting on his steps as usual, keeping an eye on the neighborhood. Jerry felt under surveillance as he cut the clover and realized, with chagrin, that although mowing could disguise the clover issues, the newly mown areas now exposed big mossy patches. Then came a brainwave! He stopped the mower and strode across to where John and his wife were both sitting in the sun, watching.

"You know, John, this year moss is IN. People actually WANT moss in their lawns. They like the variegated greens." John and his wife laughed. Jerry continued, "There's even a contest for the best moss lawn. Check it out—*mosslawns.com*."

John laughed and asked mockingly, "Oh yeah? What's the prize?"

It was time for the *coup de grâce.* "A green Miata--That's the prize. You never know. I think I've got the best moss in the area. I just might win it!" With that Jerry went back to mowing and completed the first shave of the season.

Two days later his friend Greg was to deliver the Miata before leaving on vacation. Jerry arrived home after work a quarter of an hour before five when Greg was expected to show up. John and his wife Fran were sitting out on the steps again, having Happy Hour and watching the neighbourhood. There was little time to lose.

Jerry grabbed his whipper-snipper, made a show of trimming the curb grass opposite their house, then stopped the snipper and yelled out to them, "Last minute touches before the judges arrive for the Mosslawn contest!"

John mocked, "Hey, Jerry—don't you think that's sucking up a little too much to the judges?"

"You gotta do what you gotta do," Jerry replied, "when there's a Miata to be won!"

Five minutes later, a shiny green Miata, convertible top down, drove up the street and into the Sheldons' driveway behind a hedge. Jerry raced over to Greg, explained in muted tones the hoax and enlisted his help with the deception.

"Just drive around to the side opposite these neighbours," Jerry asked him, "then park the Miata, get out, pretend to be looking at parts of the lawn, and nod your head at me when I come around the corner." To Greg's 21 year old daughter, who had come with him, Jerry handed his camera and asked her to take a picture of Greg and him standing on the lawn and shaking hands.

The timing could not have been better! The neighbours, watching incredulously, called out from their house steps, "Congratulations!"

When the Miata month had elapsed and Jerry had returned Greg's car, he sauntered casually across to talk with John, who was sitting on his stairs, having a smoke and watching the neighborhood.

"Haven't seen your sports car lately," John began.

"You know how it is," Jerry replied, "a car like that is fun for the summer, but it's no good when the fall rains come. Besides, it was getting a bit boring. I've gotten rid of it."

John was surprised, but got on to new observations about how the Sheldons' property could be improved. "Jerry, when are you goin' to chop down those overgrown hedge cedars? If you need a hand, I'll come over and do it for you." Jerry told him the offer was appreciated, but that probably they could be tidied up without cutting them down.

That was months ago. Jerry never did anything about the cedars. Last week something happened which opened his eyes a little about the neighbours.

He was working on the crèche for Sunday school. It was a crisply cool Saturday in November and the garage door was open to use the table saw out on the driveway. John and another neighbor, Hank, walked over, curious about Jerry's project. Hank's the guy who's always boasting about his workshop. If Jerry buys a tool, he's got a better brand—et cetera. You get the picture.

"So what's all the noise about?" began John. Jerry explained about the Christmas pageant and invited them to come.

"You'd like it, Hank. It'll remind you of your childhood in Winkler." Hank had told the Sheldons about his Mennonite farming roots before he left for the bright lights of Winnipeg.

"Nah—I'll pass," he said, examining the crèche. "Why don't you countersink the holes for the screws? Then you can hide them with some dowelling." Jerry thought he had pretty much finished and thought irritably about having to make changes—because of neighbours, neighbours who wouldn't mind their own business.

"It'll have to do," he said, and added lamely that he didn't have any dowelling handy.

"I've got all kinds of it!" said Hank eagerly. "No problem. I'll be back with the drills and dowelling in ten minutes." Jerry was too weary to protest. By the end of the evening, Hank had helped create an amazing crèche—one Jerry could never have made. And because he had made it, Hank decided to come to see the pageant. In fact, Hank and his wife Tanya had such a good time at last Thursday's pageant that they're talking about coming to church in the New Year!

It occurred to Jerry then that all of Hank's talk about his workshop really hadn't been about boasting; it was looking for a way to break the ice, to make friends. And his decision to come to the pageant—that happened because someone needed his help.

It reminded Jerry of Jesus asking the Samaritan woman for a drink; asking her to help him opened up the whole conversation. Maybe, just maybe, neighbours might be different if Jerry asked for their help occasionally. You know—instead of being a Lone Ranger when it comes to projects.

Once again the Christmas Bunny is blinking at the Sheldons nightly from across the cul de sac. Jerry is staring at his cedar hedge, thinking about John who rules the neighborhood. He's thinking about John's pronouncement that the cedar hedge has to go—and wondering whether, for Christmas this year, Emma might be giving him a chain saw.

"Good will to all." No doubt, that includes neighbours—you gotta love 'em!

"Who knit ya?"

Christmas in Newfoundland has some features you don't hear about in the rest of the country. For one thing, there's the tradition of dressing up in costumes, then visiting the neighbours and disguising your voice—'mummering' or 'jannying'—singing carols, getting your neighbours to guess who's behind the masks. That activity takes place during the 12 days of Christmas, between December 25th and January 6th, "Old Christmas Day". Blame the English for switching to the Gregorian calendar in 1752, but it makes for a great stretch of celebration--from the feast celebrating Nativity up to Epiphany, the feast celebrating the Coming of the Wisemen. It's community time with friends and family.

With Christmas just a few hours away, Brian has an hour to himself. He's standing by the desk in his room, wrapping gifts and listening to voices in the kitchen. A CD of Simani Christmas music is playing for the second time tonight. Simani is home-grown Newfoundland folk music. Brian's sister has flown back for Christmas from Calgary with her husband and their kids. Five year old Bella and seven year old Stevie have baked molasses cookies with their Nanny and are being instructed about what to put on the table for Santa: one of their freshly baked cookies plus a glass of watered down Purity Syrup. Soon Nan will begin her endless Christmas tales followed by suggestions about how to dress up when they go mummering on the 26th: long johns, rubber boots, garden gloves, pillowcases over their heads, lampshades for hats.

Brian has wrapped a moose puppet for his niece, and is holding the gift for his nephew. It's a Viking ship which he remembers making together with his own Uncle Stephen a generation back. To pass it on to little Stevie seems right, particularly after the events of this past year. Brian puts down the ship model and stares out at the bay. His mind drifts back over the excitement of the past year. He has uncovered something which might yet alter the fortunes of his family. A few times this year, friends have asked about his family: "Who knit ya?" We're not talking knitting needles here. When people want to understand what makes you the way you are, they ask about your parents, about who put you together—"Who knit ya?"

***

Asked that question by a fellow Newfoundlander, Brian McIvor would say his ancestors came from Cape Breton to Stormy Point on the southwest coast of Newfoundland about 1850 and the family kept up speaking Scottish Gaelic until his Dad was born in 1958. His folks were 'good hands' at the Newfoundland Railway, but couldn't see their way to much else when the narrow gauge track was torn up after 1988. Brian would sometimes walk around the Wreckhouse, where the wind was strong enough to blow cars off the 3 foot 6 inch tracks. Those were the good old days, before the closing of fish plants, before the devastation of Hurricane Igor on the east coast.

After the railway, his own family had tried a little of everything: sheep raising and vegetable farming. For a couple of months a year Brian was a deck hand on a lobster boat. The money was good for the two months, and then it was back to whatever the farm might produce that year: potatoes, turnips, carrots, beets.

Thank God for tourism! An Alabama archaeologist using satellite reconnaissance thought she had found another Viking settlement at Point Rosee, the newer name for Stormy Point--very close to the McIvor family homestead. Maybe that would prove to be a drawing card, like the Norse settlement at l'Anse aux Meadows, 600 kilometres to the north. Tourists were flying there from around the world to see a site 500 years older than Columbus. So now a Newfoundlander could get a job dressing like a Viking, or retelling sagas from Leif Eriksson or building a replica of a Viking longship.

Brian had thought he would be good at that. In High School he had researched his family connection to the Norsemen. Scottish families from the Hebrides, like his own family, descend from intermarriage of Vikings with the Gaels. He had even written to the Shetland Island Times with a description of his research project and received a sponsorship to fly from Saint John's to London, then Lerwick to attend the annual Fire Festival of Up Helly Aa. He learned that Vikings had lived in Shetland for 600 years and Danelaw had once ruled a major part of England. These were family connections which Brian was eager to explore. They might even help him get a job. Why, for all anyone knew, Brian McIvor might have Viking ancestors who settled along the coast of Newfoundland, which they called Vinland, even predating the Mi'kmaqs. It ***could*** be that the whole Codroy Valley was land originally inhabited by his own ancestors! The possibility of having ancestral rights delighted him. ***What if*** Highway 407 along the coast to Searston were shown to be on former Viking land? Or the Cape Anguille Lighthouse? Well, then—anyone on that land now . . . maybe should be paying him rent!!

He ran the idea past his friend, the MHA. (For those of us who "come from away", an MHA in Newfoundland is a Member of the House of Assembly, the provincial government.) Brian's friend, the MHA, thought his line of thinking a trifle off-kilter—"squish".

"You'd have to prove it, McIvor," said the MHA, and Brian set about just that.

From an old newspaper article, he remembered that Mary Parsons, who had a keen interest in the archaeological investigation of Stormy Point, lived in Channel/Port aux Basques. Brian phoned, introduced himself, and asked to meet her for lunch to talk about how the dig was progressing. A retired school teacher, Ms. Parsons was happy to share what she knew with another avid history buff, so Brian drove the 406 to Doyles, then headed south on the Trans Canada. Although he arrived a little early, Ms. Parsons had come earlier still and was sitting at a table, with a site map of the dig open for reference. She was short and slim with wiry white hair pulled back in a bun. Beaming, she thrust out a hand of welcome as he approached the table.

What he found out over that lunch at the hotel restaurant was well worth the hour's drive. Sarah Parcak, the Alabama archaeologist, had been excited by the discovery of a land formation pretty similar in size and shape to the longhouses at L'Anse aux Meadows up north. Unfortunately, the turf wall shape could be explained by natural processes. Still, Brian thought, how likely would it be that the size, 22 metres by 7, would occur by any natural process? Brian thanked Mary Parsons for her time, and drove back to Millville, deep in thought. He was sure that the possibility of Viking settlement could not be discounted; investigators just needed to find a few more items.

Brian took heart from the Beardmore hoax which had been remarkably successful. In 1936, an amateur gold prospector presented a few iron Viking artifacts to the Royal Ontario Museum, claiming that he had found them a few years earlier while prospecting close to Beardmore, Ontario. The museum curator was impressed by the Norse sword and axe head, had them authenticated by European experts, then bought them from James Dodd for the handsome price of $500. Then, 20 years later, the son of James Dodd admitted that his dad had found the relics in a Port Arthur basement and taken them to the site where he later claimed to find them. There was nothing intrinsically fake about these relics--they were genuine enough—except that the Vikings ***themselves*** hadn't brought them to North America. Someone else had imported them from Scandinavia in the 1920s.

Brian found the story deliciously satisfying, proof that even experts can be fooled. Perhaps *that* kind of thing could be done again at Stormy Point. A well-chosen artifact could convince people of the site until, quite possibly, genuine finds showed up later and made the fake unnecessary. So it would be a temporary proof. Put this way, it really didn't seem to be dishonest. In fact, Brian mused, he would be salvaging a genuine site from being dismissed. Already many people had said the site was too difficult for landing boats, having a rocky shore and cliffs. One good artifact could reverse that judgment.

The internet information on L'Anse aux Meadows provided a useful list of Viking artifacts. There was a whetstone, a whorl, and a cloak pin. Too difficult to reproduce, thought Brian, then his eyes lit up with the mention of iron nails discarded during boat repair. Finding those objects in Europe surely wouldn't be hard, and he began an internet search for similarly aged museum artifacts too numerous and boring to be kept on display.

Oslo and Borg in Norway, Birka in Sweden, Roskilde in Denmark—they all have Viking museum exhibits which make boat nails so commonplace that they would be relegated to backroom drawers of spare parts. Why not borrow a few? They'd never be missed. How many would one need? Would a museum employee be interested in making a few bucks? Then, quite unexpectedly, Brian came across an eBay ad for genuine Viking era nails, apparently gleaned from sites in Scandinavia. 'It's possible,' he thought. "You can buy Roman coins." So why wouldn't someone try to flog a few lousy Viking nails on eBay? The photos online looked pretty similar to what had been excavated at L'Anse aux Meadows. Brian passed his computer cursor over the image, magnifying to the limit, and marveled, grinning, at the pitted, rusty iron. You could purchase three nails for a hundred dollars from an Ontario dealer who would have them sent within a week from Scotland. He could not believe his luck and made the online purchase immediately.

In the following days Brian roamed the excavation area, planning where it might be best to "discover" the nails. Perhaps beside the burned boulder, or in the pile of sifted dirt, or beside a steep trail approaching the beach, or from an unexcavated mound on the old McIvor sheep pasture, not far from the longhouse shaped earthwork. He settled on the last as the safest bet.

As he awaited delivery of his package from Scotland, Brian was not idle. He phoned a member of the Area Development Association and asked to meet to discuss "a valley development issue". Harald Penney was just heading over to the Codroy Community Hall to help plan the annual Fire Department fund-raising lobster dinner, and invited Brian to drop by his own house right after the meeting. Coffee got brewing and Brian began. He explained that if, as he suspected, his own family were descended from the Viking colony which settled in Point Rosee, then the McIvors were in a special category. It was a case of reclaiming original land—or coming to some kind of monetary agreement with those who now occupied that land. He wouldn't be greedy, he said, but would expect a token 10% of any income from those properties which now were occupied by others.

Harald Penney listened with confused interest, then alarm, but waited for Brian to finish. From a backpack Brian drew a Minnesota Vikings baseball cap and pointed to the team symbol of a fierce horned warrior. "Since this is Viking country, why not have the RCMP wear Viking helmets as part of the local force? They could keep the normal RCMP uniform, but wear the helmets and have a similar picture on the squad cars. What do you think?"

Penney was clearly uncomfortable. "You real sure your family dates back to the Viking colony? We don't even know yet for sure that Point Rosee had Vikings."

"Yes b'y. I'm that sure. As for the proof, I think we're coming really close. Any day now, with these excavations . . ." Brian's voice trailed off with a sense of premonition.

"Well," said Penney uncertainly, "That's not the kind of thing we deal with in the Development Association. Anything to do with the RCMP—mind now, that's federal."

Brian smiled confidently. "No doubt it'll all take a while to sort out. Thanks for your time, Harald. Hope your lobster dinner planning went well. You know," he said, as he got up from the table and made his way to the door, "about the lobster catch—fishing seasons might not apply to the Vikings and their descendants. Now wouldn't ***that*** be interesting! Fresh lobster all year 'round, like the guys down in Maine and New Hampshire. I might even open a store."

Harald Penney didn't know quite how to respond, hastily opened the door for his guest to depart and nervously mumbled his usual goodbye: "Take care."

The package from Glasgow arrived by courier 10 days after his online order. He opened the bubble wrap carefully and extracted three nails, individually wrapped in gauze. An accompanying terse typed note read: "Authentic Viking Nails found at Scandinavian sites." The nails were as good as the photos--square, of different lengths, bent unevenly and authentically rusty. Brian grinned, rolled them up in a tea towel, and headed off with his shovel to the old sheep pasture. At the mound, he wondered what reason he might offer for digging and chancing upon the nails. It seemed a logical place for a drainage trench, so he began a trench from one dip in the landscape toward a lower dip on another side of the mound.

Quite by surprise, as the trench approached the mound, his shovel struck an old wooden plank and Brian knew with excitement that his nails had found a home. He removed all three carefully from the towel and rolled each in the dirt of his trench. One nail he forced into dirt under the wood he had encountered, leaving only the head visible. Another nail he pushed into rotten wood, again with its head showing. The third he rolled up again in the towel and headed home.

Mary Parsons, when he phoned her, was keen enough to drive from Port aux Basques to see the nail and the mound where he had found it. They wandered together past an excavation pit and the piles of sifted earth and onto the old sheep pasture, where he showed her his drainage trench and the mysterious mound. It was gratifying when she spotted one of the nails and removed it gingerly, marveling at the square shape.

"You're right," she admitted. "It's the right kind of nail, just like the ones at L'Anse aux Meadows. I'll let the team know." Mary looked at him, eyes bulging. "If you can believe this, they'd given up!"

"Really?" asked Brian, incredulous.

And within the next two weeks a team of university students was installed, gridding the mound and preparing for action. Brian wandered around, pleased, wearing his Minnesota Vikings baseball cap. One of the young archaeology students told him that the picture on the hat was wrong, that Vikings didn't really have horns or wings on their helmets. This was irritating, but Brian ignored the student and wore his cap proudly, knowing that vindication was not far off. Sure enough, the third nail was found almost immediately, adding to excitement. Rotting boards were gently brushed off and labelled for their locations in the grid.

Then, about a week into the dig, a rusty can and broken china plate were unearthed. Bit by bit it became apparent that the mound, at least a good part of it, was the remains of an outhouse, possibly 100 to 150 years old.

"But what about the nails?" asked Mary, taken aback that she had called in the team.

An expert re-examined the three nails and concluded that they had been cast in molds, not manufactured from smelted bog iron. He pointed out where the seams had been ground off along the nail shanks.

Well! As they say when you can feel a storm approaching, that was a brewer!

Mary turned to Brian, whose dismay was certainly genuine. "Someone has played a horrible trick on you!"

Brian nodded earnestly. "Yes—a horrible trick!"

To add insult to injury, the MHA had dropped by that day to witness the dig, and stood by, gloating.

"Well, McIvor, it seems you're outta luck. When do you think you'll be proving your ancestors landed here a millennium ago? When exactly do you think you'll be collecting rent from the Codroy Valley?"

Brian's thoughts were scrambled, but dreams die hard. He hadn't been careful enough with the nails, but that didn't mean genuine bog iron nails couldn't be obtained, perhaps next time from Iceland.

"You're wanting to know when?" he repeated dazed, then folded his arms and announced with defiance, "Now the once." Which is to say, without getting too specific, "soon enough."

The MHA guffawed. "Brian McIvor, whoever knit ya dropped a stitch!"

That was back in August. It's December now and he feels less confident. It is indeed time to pass on this Viking ship to a new generation.

Brian can hear the carol singing going on still in the kitchen: "I saw three ships come sailing in on Christmas Day in the morning."

Ironic, he muses. His own ship has not come in—and is unlikely to.

Last Sunday the minister said the three ships of the carol referred to ships of the desert— camels, bearing gifts for the newborn king. The minister said that even the magi couldn't outgive the Giver, the One who gives life itself, the One who gave His Son.

With the joy of Christmas singing in the kitchen, mistakes of the past year don't seem to matter much. Brian feels thankful—for life, for being a Newfoundlander, for family, for a New Year and a fresh start, for Christmas. It's a gift—and maybe his own gifts are a way of giving something back. Like the Magi, he's come to pay his dues. He senses there may be a better answer, a more profound answer, to the question, "Who knit ya?"

All God's Creatures

Francis of Assisi is credited with beginning the tradition of singing Christmas carols in one's own language, rather than switching to Latin to sing about holy things. 'Gloria in excelsis Deo' continues to form part of our repertoire, but thanks to Francis, we are saved the ignominy of having to explain to our children that we do not know what we are singing about. Thank you, St. Francis! He liked to make things simple. No doubt that was why he began the crèche scenes—to help people imagine that holy night.

And it was this wonderful fellow who, 800 years ago, reminded the Christian world that all of God's creation, not just humans, sings praise to God.

The Christmas crèche scenes all show farm animals crowding around the babe in the manger and we sing "ox and ass before him bow". Is that just figuratively speaking, or might that actually have happened? A friend of ours tells of one of her practice sessions with her stand-up harp, a day when deer had come out of the forest into her yard. She opened the sliding door and continued to play, delighted to see that the deer settled down on the grass. Best of all, when her performance was over, a stag approached her and bowed his antlered head before retreating with the others to the forest.

Well . . . if the stones can cry out and the trees of the field can clap their hands, and if Balaam's donkey could reprimand the prophet, is it too much to think that another donkey was somehow aware of someone very special she was carrying to Bethlehem . . . or thirty years later—the colt which had never been ridden, willingly submissive to the Lord of all Creation riding him into Jerusalem?

What of that day or night when Jesus was born? Did the animals in the stable sense the presence of God? John writes in the Revelation that he heard every creature joining in with the praise. Perhaps St. Francis thought of this when he called the birds his 'little sisters'. They are all God's creatures.

***

On every property they have owned, Jerry and Emma Sheldon have set up a bird feeder. When I say "owned", I am loosely referring to properties for which they have had a mortgage—but that's another story. The point here is, they like watching wild birds of all types come to visit their feeder, placed strategically close to a kitchen nook. Usually it's a family of Black-Capped Chickadees, or a flock of Purple Finches, or a couple of Juncos, or a whole clan of yellow-green Pine Siskins. Occasionally there's a silent swoop of a larger Flicker or a squawking Stellar Jay muscling in on the sunflower seeds. It's all God's creation and they rejoice in having ringside seats. Close to their kitchen table the Sheldons keep a guide to birds of the Pacific Northwest so they can identify unusual visitors—Lincoln Sparrows, Gold-Crowned Kinglets, maybe a Cedar Waxwing.

When Jerry and Emma first moved to Langley, B.C., their neighbours—those who expressed an opinion—were less than enthusiastic about bird feeders, claiming they would attract rats. Since the existence of a feeder in the neighbourhood was frowned upon, Jerry hid their feeder by planting a row of pyramid cedars between them and the neighbours who might otherwise have objected. To deal with the eventuality of rodents, he placed the little house-shaped feeder on a pole six feet above ground level, and fashioned a squirrel guard out of aluminum flashing. This cone-shape was attached just below the feeder, preventing squirrels, rats or cats from molesting the bird friends. The neighbour's black feline slunk on her white mittened paws into the yard, tail twitching, eyes alert for action at the feeder or the bird bath and for the occasional bird hopping around picking up crumbs. The Sheldons lost one or two birds that way, but in general birds were too skittish to be caught unaware. Moreover, Emma took to storming out of the house, shooing away the cat whenever she spotted it.

All went well for a few months, with their daily private viewing of wild birds. Then, when Jerry was feeling quite smug about avoiding detection, he and Emma both saw with horror that a rat had somehow scaled their new cedar hedge and leapt across onto the wooden feeder. There he was, hunched on the feeding platform, nibbling contentedly! Jerry was incensed! The squirrel guard had not been enough. Worse, the Sheldons were guilty of harbouring a criminal!

Furious, Jerry moved smoothly and unobtrusively out of view, then stealthily made his way to the garage where he picked out a shovel and crept around the house. Shovel poised above his head, he inched forward and slammed his weapon down on the unsuspecting rat. Success! Another swat or two to the critter on the patio and there was no more rat. Unfortunately, there was no more feeder either! Broken pieces of the structure lay around him.

This actually proved to be a good thing, since the next feeder was a plastic tube affair dangling from an iron hook, still fixed to the original pole, but now impossible for any rat to jump onto without sliding off. Some research also revealed that shelled sunflower seeds created less 'fall out' for ground feeders. So Jerry and Emma were soon off to the races with a better set-up.

Mention of their rat escapade to a friendly neighbour resulted in laughter and some unexpected information—or was it advice?

Apparently, rats also slurp up water from fish ponds. Yes—the Sheldons have a fish pond, painstakingly dug, landscaped, restocked every spring with more goldfish to compensate for the ones fished out by herons or raccoons. Jerry is proud of the water pump set up with a burbling spring coming out of a stone. It took him a long time with an old electric drill and a concrete bit to bore through that stone. "So," he says, "the pond stays."

Occasionally, in the dead of night, Jerry would awaken to a scurrying sound in the walls. With a heavy heart, he bought several of the classic rat traps, screwed them to small boards to prevent any traps from being dragged away, baited them with peanut butter and ventured up into the attic through a trap door in the closet. Within days he had trapped two or three rats—not the nasty city variety which one imagines have been up all night playing poker, but the relatively clean country types with smooth grey coats. Clearly, he had a responsibility to the neighbourhood to discourage the vermin squatters. It occurred to him that outside traps might work, but cats and birds might also be hurt. How could one avoid injuring other animals?

Someone advised Jerry that live squirrel traps would solve the problem, so he baited a squirrel cage and positioned it close to the cedar hedge and the feeder. Sure enough, a few days later a cute little guy timidly looked out from the cage. This posed a new problem. Live traps are humane, not hurting the animals, but the customers do require relocation. Jerry trundled out to his car with the caged critter and put it in the trunk for its first car ride. Their home in Langley Township is not far from farmland, but he hesitated to inflict another rat on any farm. His drive south continued to the border, where he parked, took out his guest in its cage and hopped a ditch to a border marker. And there Jerry Sheldon gave the rat the choice of citizenship: did he want to remain Canadian, or to try his luck in the States? He shook the rat out on the grass, watched it uncertainly scamper south, then hurried to his car, wondering whether a border guard might have seen the dirty deed—dreading also the possibility that he might see the rat in a side mirror loping after the car as it sped home.

Jerry determined to stop the blighters from getting into their attic and wandered around the house looking for ways rats might access the roof. One obvious trellis had to be cut shorter and for a time it seemed this had worked. Then, one sunny afternoon, he spied a rat nimbly make its way along a honeysuckle stem onto the roof despite the missing trellis support. It was unbelievable! Out came the ladder and the honeysuckle and ivy were cut well back.

Still, rats in the attic have continued to be caught every few weeks. Jerry suspects where they get in, but he is reluctant to cut down plants which beautify the home—a tall hedge of cedars less than a foot from the roof and a wisteria vine which curls up the front pillars and along toward the gutters. The exterminator guy has pointed these out during his weekly Rat Patrol. Jerry is still thinking about options. Emma says it would be great if this Christmas 'not a creature was stirring, not even a mouse'—or a rat.

Recently the Sheldons were invited to a barbecue next door and were enjoying conversation when there was a shriek from another guest who had seen a rat running along a fence rail. In the pandemonium and consternation which ensued, Jerry glanced at his wife with a grin. This problem was no news to the two of them and they chuckled. “That's George,” said Jerry matter-of-factly to the neighbours. “If you name them, they're not so bad.” He explained that some African rats from Gambia are named, trained and taken to Cambodia for an important mission: locating millions of buried land mines. Little packs have been fitted to their backs and they are let out on leashes to sniff out the buried TNT. "In fact," Jerry continued, "they're so good at it that each trained rat can check out an area of 2000 square feet in just 20 minutes—leaps and bounds ahead of dogs or humans! Why, these creatures probably deserve the Nobel Peace Prize!" The neighbours didn't seem moved by the thought of rats performing this great service for mankind. He tried.

Sooner or later, the wisteria vine will have to be severely cut back, and the cedars next to the Sheldons' roof will have to be sawn down. But the pond stays and losing the feeder is out of the question. They've never been fond of cats, but . . . maybe they'll stop discouraging the neighbour's cat from trespassing. In fact, Emma admits—blessings on the cat they used to scowl at! That squirrel caught this morning munching on a tomato plant—she might decide the risk is too great if she sees the little panther roaming around. Losing a bird or two to the cat police must be weighed against letting the varmints know that Sheldon property is off-limits. Emma says it's the law of the wild which we all accept when we lose goldfish to the raccoons or herons. "All God's creatures got a place in the choir." So goes the song, and if there's a whisker of truth to it, rats have a place, too.

It's Christmas and the Sheldons are feeling charitable. After all, the Apostle Paul does say that all creation groans for God to come and set right a world gone wrong. If animals can sense a coming storm or know somehow which humans to trust, can't they sense when the Son of God is breathing the same stable air and evil is fleeing?—that calls for a bark of joy, or a moo of satisfaction, a particularly cheerful birdsong . . . or an excited squeak from the rodent gallery. "And Heaven and nature sing!" "Let everything that has breath praise the Lord."

Merry Christmas to ALL God's creatures!

To this magnanimous blessing, the Sheldons add a prayer for themselves. When Christmas is over, they ask, wouldn't it be nice if George would pack up the family and set out for the land of opportunity south of the border?

Beyond

The Bridge

Tulemun was located on a bay at the end of a five mile inlet of the island, a fiord well stocked with sea life. Originally a fishing community of about 2000, less than half that number remained. At the beginning of the conflicts, many young people had been conscripted and families relocated for work in cities on the continent—a tragic choice in hindsight.

Those who stayed in Tulemun had envied city life, dreamt of someday visiting Vancouver, maybe even flying to Paris, London, Tokyo, Beijing, New York—but these were all gone now, their accomplishments remembered and discussed by grandparents. A few had actually been there, seen the lights, and heard the gas powered cars. They had no gas, apart from one dwindling tank reserved for generators, or any clue of how to make it.

Ernest's father said the villagers were lucky, fortunate to have survived nuclear devastation, perhaps the last ones to be standing when the smoke cleared. Well, they thought themselves the only ones until the journey. The people of Tulemun were lucky to live far enough north that their little town was well away from the direct hits taken by major centers. So they limped on after the war, generators continuing to run the lights until the bulbs burned out, the generators seized up, or the last drops of gas had gone, then they were reduced to what all understood in the way of technology—embarrassingly simple.

Huddled below a Spruce forest, the village was picturesque, a half-moon bay lined with old buildings built with brick or river rock. Beyond a seaside meadow and up a gentle slope were meandering lanes of small wooden clapboard houses, all capped with slate roof tiles. From four piers along the waterfront, ramps with handrails descended to docks where little fishing boats, small clinker dinghies, bobbed up and down. A couple of trawlers, with no gas for their engines, had been tied up for good a decade ago and became houseboats. At low tides, the sea level dropped several meters, exposing a mud bar pockmarked by geoducks, those enormous burrowing clams which were now part of their food supply. With the smell of the sea and the sound of squawking gulls, it was possible to forget that any outside world existed. On good days (and there were many), life in Tulemun looked idyllic.

But the land seemed to be sinking. For one thing, Market Square, built on the meadow, was under a few inches of water each year. When they were taught about the water cycle, the teacher explained that Market Square being flooded was just a seasonal phenomenon caused by spring run-off when the snows melted. That didn't explain why the base of the statue was now permanently under water or why the basements of some older houses were half full of water all year round.

Cousin Harriet's family had one of those houses in Old Town. As far back as Ernie's first form, he remembers that relatives would come to her house for harvest celebration and the cousins would all sleep in the "under-kitchen", the half-floor storage bin. Even then the true basement was unusable, water up to the three foot mark. Aunt Jo was adamant about children not opening the basement access door. That was locked eventually, but adults forgot about the access from the under-kitchen, so it was an annual adventure for the cousins to take a pitch torch and explore the murky recesses. They huddled together with Ernie's older sister Judith protesting, but going with the others anyway, the whole time anxiously reminding everyone that it would serve them right if the hatch swung shut and they couldn't get out. But they dared each other on, wading chest deep through the frigid water, feeling along the rock until Harriet or Ernie or the youngest, Peter, touched slugs and recoiled in delighted horror to the under-kitchen.

There was the Fall Ernie tricked Peter into going first, then meanly closed the hatch on him, holding it shut until he threatened to tell his father about the opening. Ernie pulled the hatch open right away then. Peter crawled out, blubbering, red-faced, pushing the older boy away with his pudgy hands. He told Aunt Jo anyway and that was the end of any children being allowed in the under-kitchen.

Years later, when Harriet had her seventeenth birthday party, Ernest helped with the kitchen clean-up and remembered about the access. It was blocked then with an old commode-turned-china cabinet. Curiosity outweighed fear of Aunt Jo who was occupied in the hall with guests, showing them the family gallery of paintings. Ernie worked the heavy cabinet inch by inch from the wall until he could pull the hatch partly open. Light from the kitchen lamps glimmered on something inside and he realized that the floor joists of the underkitchen were now touching water too.

Ernest suspected, even then. Newer houses had no basements, so the builders probably knew, although they wouldn't talk about it. Maybe they reasoned that if they didn't mention it, the problem might disappear someday, like a puddle evaporating in the heat of a summer day.

The Pederson family would be all right, Ernie's father said, as long as they remembered to do things in fours. God would help them if they did things in fours, he said, because God blesses the number four. There are four seasons. Animals have four legs. Insects have four wings and four stages of metamorphosis—egg, larva, pupa and adult. There are four chambers of the heart. It's inherent in the way we were created! No wonder, then, that humans choose to make rectangular bricks, tables and houses. No wonder that humans make furniture with four legs, or violins with four strings, or even mark music with four beats in common time. Of course rooms have four walls! That's why there were four piers built for the harbor. According to the Writing which they all grew up with, Truth must be proclaimed to the four points of the compass. Also the Teacher had said, "Do not speak to one side what you will not also speak to the other." So in the daily declaration, they stood together and called out the creed to the four directions, as they faced north, then south, then east and west. And they called out each article of faith four times. Ernie's own family was particularly careful to deal with Truth this way, performing the declaration four times a day—at daybreak, noon, evening meal and bedtime. In this way, they could be sure to have thoroughly obeyed the teaching.

Ben told Ernie privately that the declaration was a misunderstanding of the teaching that people needed to share Truth with people around, no matter where they came from—this is what was meant by the Teacher when he said to speak to all points of the compass.

"Don't you believe that four is the number blessed by God?" Ernie asked him.

Rather than giving a straight answer, Ben asked to see Ernie's hand. He put down the pencil he was holding on the table beside them, then took Ernie's hand in his, turning it palm up.

"How many fingers are there?"

"Four," the boy replied.

"Now, would you pass me my pencil, please," Ben requested.

As soon as Ernie had picked up the pencil, Ben reached out swiftly and held his wrist.

"Never forget that four fingers need the thumb, Ernie. Our four fingers stay together as good friends, but until the thumb meets them, it is hard for them to accomplish much." Ernie looked down at the way he was holding the pencil between his thumb and the other fingers. Was Ben saying that the holy number should be five?

Ben was ten years older. He was a slight, sinewy young man, not much taller than Ernie, with wiry black hair. He was quiet, studious, but with a gentle humour. The Council had recognized his gifts in building and employed him for maintenance work. That was why Ernie went so often to the Town Maintenance building, to watch Ben drafting bridges or house renovations. Early on it became his dream to be like Ben.

When Ernie finished Basic Education, at age fourteen, his father got him into apprenticeship with Town Maintenance and it was then the youth realized how the problem had worsened. One ancient restaurant was half submerged; water was half way up the windows of the first floor and the building tilted slightly toward the sea. Council had decided to try to save the rest of Founders' Row—a general trading store and a pioneer hostel. Floating slabs had already begun to replace fixed foundation walls, but Maintenance insisted that heavy buildings like those of Founders' Row could only be saved by dismantling them rock by rock and relocating them on high ground. During this time an interesting discovery was made.

Where pieces of shoreline had washed away were what appeared to be pilings. Under the buildings too they could see cut ends of cedar tree trunks five to six feet in diameter and packed tightly together. At first, the trunks were thought to support the buildings only, but as more and more salvage work was done, it could be seen that pilings probably extended under the entire shoreline area. It appeared as though much of the settlement had been constructed on a massive underground structure of columns which now was slowly sinking into the sea bottom.

The discovery didn't change what had to be done. The solution was still to move endangered buildings to higher ground—or abandon them. And Ernie was content enough with the job apart from an incident which happened in his first month.

As with any unoccupied structures, recycling resulted in stocks of nails, bolts, windows and other hardware which could be reused in new construction. About a week after Ernie had been taken on as a member of the salvage crew, some rare cabinet doors disappeared from the stockroom, and Fred Baker, his boss, suspected him of the theft. Eventually an older crew member, Glen Toller, owned up. Toller told Fred that he had "borrowed" the items to check whether or not they would fit in cabinets he was making. He would, of course, be happy to bring other items to make up for the doors which he simply "had to have". Fred gruffly accepted this explanation. He never did apologize to Ernie for accusing him, but did treat the boy well after that rough start.

Crew members were well recompensed, accumulating "Tulemun barter credit" with the Town Clerk, and the relocation of buildings was both challenging and satisfying. It was clear that there would probably be salvage work for the rest of Ernie's life, if he wanted it.

There are always prophets of doom who seize on odd facts, predicting the worst possible scenario. Fred Baker, Ernie's boss, became quite religious. At lunch breaks he would tell his employee the latest he had heard from the Seer. Within one generation it would happen—they would all sink into the sea, and if people believed this, they should prepare for the end.

"How?" Ernie was somewhat interested.

"The Seer says there's a better land and it's not sinking—prepared for us all just like this one was at one time. We can all move there if we want." The Pederson family had already built on Morgan's Hill; Ernie felt pretty secure and said so.

But he did ask Ben what he thought of this. Ben's reply was enigmatic. "Ernie, the Seer is right, but the better question is, what do we do about it?"

"All right," Ernie challenged him, "if you know, tell me."

"It's not something easy to hear," Ben replied. "It's better if I show you. Can you come with me tomorrow to Founders' Row?"

The boy's interest was piqued. "Sure. What time?"

"Meet me here at eight. We'll be gone all day, but you won't need a lunch."

The next day Ernie arrived early at Ben's office in the Town Maintenance Building. Ben arrived a few minutes before eight with four members of the Salvage Team and two wheelbarrows full of tools. Ernie expressed surprise at the arrival of these young men he often worked with, then off they went to the pioneer hostel on Founders' Row. There all were introduced to Mr. Allister, the old owner/manager of the hostel, who led the group over to a kitchen table to meet an even older couple seated there.

"This here's Mikey and his wife Aida who've run the kitchen since before I arrived. So, of course, this is their home still. Some of the fishermen live here when they're not out with the boats—and they do what they can by contributing fish. We've never turned away a family looking for meals when the crops are bad." Mr. Allister seemed overwhelmed by Ben's offer to help, and his preamble was almost an apology.

"You know I can't pay for this," he began, but Ben quickly motioned him to say no more.

"Show us the beds, tables and chairs," said Ben, "We'll begin with those."

It became apparent that the whole team was there, Ernie included, to help move the hostel furniture to higher ground, though where, exactly, none of them knew. No one asked, but worked in twos to lift and remove the beds, following Ben, who had two stacked chairs in his arms. The rest followed, uncertain of where he was going, until he led the group into the Town Maintenance Building and into the meeting room, where he got everyone to deposit the load. Then he directed them to set up the beds like a dormitory. Back and forth all morning they lugged items until the meeting room was quite full. The old kitchen couple shambled along with Mr. Allister as the last of their possessions was taken to the new location.

"Could I offer you some lunch?" asked Aida. "I have apples, cheese and some bread. Water, of course. Sorry there isn't more." Her husband Mikey opened a basket he had brought with them and offered it hesitatingly.

"That'll be just fine," said Ben, and helped the old man put the food out on plates to bring to the workers as they all flopped down on the floor, leaning against the walls. When everyone had been served, Ben himself found a place to sit with a napkin of food. Mr. Allister was evidently waiting for this moment when he could present something privately to Ben. Sheltered in the coat he had been carrying was an eight by ten inch black and white photo, framed and under glass. He took this from the coat and carefully handed it to Ben.

“The six people in this photo were the Founders and first Council of Tulemun. The photo has hung over the fireplace mantle in our dining room from before my time. I can’t pay for all the work you’ve done today to save parts of the hostel, but I’d like you to have this.” Ben rose and hugged Mr. Allister, then gently held the photo examining it while the old manager, pleased, looked on.

“I’ve seen pictures of Arthur Knox,” said Ben. “Isn’t that him on the right of the group?”

Mr. Allister was delighted. “You’ve a good eye!”

“It’s a lovely gift,” said Ben. “It’s an honour to receive it. Will you allow me to choose a place in the village where others apart from me will see and appreciate it?”

The old man nodded, beaming.

Following the meal, Ben showed to the crew some cupboards which he had them dismantle and carry up to the Town Maintenance Building. Until this time they hadn't run into anyone, but now they encountered a group of Town Councillors, aghast that their meeting room had been set up to act as a make-shift lodging, and livid that Ben had done this without permission.

"Not only so," said one angry councillor, "but Allister told us himself that he couldn't pay for the Salvage Team. What on earth do you think you're doing?"

Ben was quiet, but firm. "We have always maintained that Council exists to serve the community. Here is the test. Do we prefer our own comfort when others are sinking? To whom does the building really belong?" They were furious, but tongue-tied. It was clear the councillors resented Ben, yet they could not easily say anything with Mr. Allister walking up to the group.

“By the way,” added Ben, as the old man joined them, “Mr. Allister has brought from the hostel an unusual photo of our Founders, the first Council which included Arthur Knox. Isn’t he the great grandfather of our current Chair? Well, that wonderful museum photo is a gift to hang up in the Council Meeting Room.”

Ben handed the framed photo to one of the councilors and turned swiftly towards Mr. Allister, who stood close by, somewhat confused and speechless.

“Thank you, Mr. Allister, for this historic photo—a perfect addition to the room where our Council meets today!”

Within a month, Council had found an alternate location for the hostel, and was able to return the meeting room to its original function. But Ben got away with this, and Ernie’s admiration for him grew.

***

Much of the village did sink as years went by, and Ernest, now sixteen, was grateful to learn building skills beside older trades-men. People bartered, paid in kind with their skills, hunting, fishing, farm produce, or sheer labour. Houses at the bottom of Morgan's Hill began to experience some problems, but the Pederson home was close to the top and Ernie wasn't concerned. Sometime the sinking would have to stop.

It was a bit much when relocated buildings began to go under again. Council decided to let them go this time, and people noticed monthly how their pioneer past slipped more and more out of sight.

Many abandoned the houses which they could neither rescue nor sell, and moved inland to a new and growing village. People there actually went back to digging basements until someone reported running into cedar posts. Predictably, they were five or six feet across, packed tightly together and the tops of them could be found wherever a hole went down ten feet. Nowhere was the earth and rock found to be deeper than ten feet! A meeting was held in Newtown. No one, not even today, they said, could hope to form a foundation of pilings sufficient to hold up such a large area. The existence of these pilings pointed to some great former civilization having engineered this. Religious types like Fred Baker said that such a feat was beyond human ability. Shirley McFarland, the Science teacher, responded that what they had been calling pilings were actually tree trunks of a primeval forest preserved by the mud. Perhaps some natural catastrophe had sheared them all off at ground level. "In any event," she laughed, "you can be sure that the whole island is not resting on pilings. What we've found here is sure to be a local phenomenon."

These explanations seemed reasonable enough. Newtown continued to grow and the troubles of the shoreline village didn't touch most families in the inland location. The Pederson family, too, had moved from Morgan's Hill since all the approaches to their old house were now under water. All the furnishings had had to be ferried across for the move. Afterwards, Ernie's father, Simon Pederson, had been able to rent their house to some artists who didn't mind rowing across to the main island to bring weekly payments in the form of eggs and vegetables.

Once the move had been made, the Pedersons settled into Newtown, happy to begin again. In the new settlement there was renewed hope, much laughter, the daily sounds of hammers and handsaws, families playing and working together. Ernie walked half an hour daily to the coast where salvage work provided steady employment.

Newtown, or Newton, was pleasantly situated, nestled in a valley between the inland hills. Grain and fruit grew well there. That is, until the farms themselves began to become marshland. There was little to account for it. Spring run-off had not been unusually heavy. Seasonal rains had been more or less the same. People found that the marsh water was salty, even after filtration, and many began to suspect it was sea water seeping in.

"Why not look for higher ground, move away from the sea entirely?" Young Ernie had come to a meeting of the Council and posed his question.

The answer he expected came first. "Our food supply is dependent on fishing. It would be difficult to find an alternative to salmon."

Surprisingly, Ben, who rarely spoke up in these meetings, took his side. "Ernie is right to bring this up. Survival is more important than diet."

A few councillors looked uncomfortably at each other, then at the Chair, Sarena Knox. She was a no-nonsense woman, a female version of her great grandfather in the photo on the wall. Sarena spoke for the rest: "There is another reason, one we rarely mention, but equally important. We suspect that those responsible for the Great Retaliation may still be alive and may eventually come looking for other survivors. Then we shall finally have the chance to pay them back as they deserve. If we move inland, we may miss our opportunity."

Most councillors looked away from Ernie or at their feet, but Ben spoke again, this time directly to the Chair. Ernie expected his shrewd friend to point out the obvious, that a few hundred survivors from the war were in no position to attack or even defend themselves from invaders with sophisticated weapons. To his surprise, Ben focused on something quite different.

"This is not the intended way. You have learned nothing from the wars. Desire for retaliation is a vicious cycle which must stop. It stops with me."

The words were carefully, slowly articulated. He did not sound angry, but more tired and resigned. Then, in the silence which followed, he rose from the table and walked out of the room, leaving the door open as he went. Ernie watched his friend, and then followed him out of the Council chamber to see where he might be going. Close to where parts of the old Founders' Row lay submerged, Ernie caught up with his friend, who was gazing out at a squall on the water.

"What did you mean—'It stops with me'?" It sounded ominous as he repeated Ben's words and Ernie dreaded the reply.

Ben waited a moment, then began. "You remember the Greek legend of Pandora's jar, the *pithos* from which she allowed so much evil to escape?"

Ernie nodded.

His friend continued. "As the story goes, once released, evil escaped in all directions, impossible to recapture, a threat forever. It is a good warning, but it suggests, does it not, that evil can no longer be reined in, that now it will multiply and poison all of creation—like spilled black ink, rapidly staining everything."

Ernie listened, feeling nervous and expectant.

"But Ernie, my friend, there is another ending." Ben chuckled. "All of the poison which has funneled out into the world I pull back into myself. I suck the poison from the viper's bite. You see, I am the blotting paper. I have the power to absorb the flow. Do you believe this, Ernie?”

Ernie nodded eagerly. But actually, he understood only vaguely what he was hearing.

***

As fear of flooding settled on Newton, there was a strange sense also of what to do about it. It was not the sensible building of dams or even moving to higher ground, but an uncanny certainty that nothing would suffice short of full scale evacuation to the eastern hills. At this time, one of the villagers, a young farmer named Sammy Schmidt, had dreams of a great line of people crossing a bridge to safety. It was a recurring dream which he spoke about often and with urgency. The bridge in his dream apparently had four towers visible before being engulfed at its far end in mist. Sammy's mention of 'four' was enough to sway some elders who felt that God must be in such a vision of rescue—whether it would find literal or symbolic fulfilment. Given the seal of approval, Sammy's dream of the bridge gave hope and villagers began to speak of 'the land beyond the bridge'.

Ben, in all of the discussion, was annoyingly silent. He kept to himself. After each day at his Township job, he visited someone struggling with the heart-breaking decision of what to do about a home sinking, what should be salvaged, how to prepare for the journey inland. One day Ernie asked Ben directly about the Bridge.

"Is there such a thing?"

"Oh, yes," Ben replied without hesitation. "You can be sure of that. If the Creator allows our land to sink, of course He has planned an escape. And there is always something better where we are going."

"But how do we find the Bridge? Is it strong enough to hold everyone? What of the weak and the elderly who cannot walk far?"

Ben looked at Ernie closely and smiled warmly. "How do the salmon find their way back to their birth streams after spending their lives in the ocean?"

Enough of elementary science came back to Ernie for him to offer an answer. "They smell something familiar in the stream and follow until they can go no farther."

"Exactly so, my friend. We will sense in our hearts the way to travel, then we must go without knowing the rest."

The town planner seemed unwilling to continue the conversation and Ernie did not press him.

***

It became clear to Town Council, over several weeks, that Ben McAdams was working at cross purposes to their own. They were anxious to quell fears of the citizens, while their colleague daily urged people to prepare to evacuate. Speaking to Ben about this dissension did not result in his compliance, but seemed to stir him to more ardent efforts, directing people to select only what would be needed on the journey. If the trend continued, there would be few villagers left to run the stores or maintain life as they knew it. This baffled, then frustrated the Council who called him to account in a special meeting. The Council Chair, Serena, summed up their feelings in a way they could all support.

"Ben, we applaud your care for our citizens and we, like you, think it is a good thing to talk about a bridge. But it is a bridge of the mind, a hope for a brighter future which we can surely achieve if we all stick together here. You are undermining the way of life which the Creator intended by putting us here and keeping us through the Great Retaliation."

Ben politely disagreed. "We are deluding ourselves if we think we are not called to the journey." So they fired him. But it made no difference to how he went about his help of citizens distraught over their slowly sinking structures.

Ernie was astounded that Ben went on with life nonchalantly, never speaking badly of the Council. He wanted to talk about this even if Ben could quietly keep his composure.

"It's so unfair! You've gone out of your way to help people—and now they fire you!"

They were in Ben's kitchen and Ben looked over from the eel-grass he was cutting up, but didn't reply immediately. He filled two bowls, sprinkled black huckleberries over them both, and passed a bowl of the salad to his young friend. Then he sat opposite with his own bowl and said a prayer of thanks. Normally, Ernie would have begun his salad right away. He loved the taste of herring spawn mixed with sweet grass and berries. But this situation with Ben's firing so rankled him that he waited impatiently for a response. "Well . . . aren't you going to tell the community what Council has done? They should be held to account!"

Ben savoured a mouthful of the salad and looked thoughtful.

"Remember when your boss accused you wrongly of stealing. Did you forgive him?"

"Yes."

"Why?"

Ernie considered this. "I make mistakes, too, and I hope others will forgive me when I do."

Ben nodded. "Good thinking, Ernie! It's something like the barter credit you have banked with the Town Clerk, saving for the day you will need to use it. But there is a debt which people cannot pay by using the barter system."

Ernie chewed slowly, waiting for Ben to explain.

"The Creator owes nothing to any person, but gives life to all. This we can never repay, but he is pleased when we choose to bless and not curse his creation, to be peace-makers."

Ernie could sense where this was heading. "But it takes two people to make peace. You are only one, and the Council is not looking for peace with you."

Ben smiled.

"You misunderstand. The Creator who wants peace with all is one peace-maker. I am the other, who asks the Creator to forgive others. This is the way to renew life, but in the end—you are right, people have to want life. And when the root is bad, grafting is required to save the rest of the tree."

Ernie looked puzzled and Ben pointed to an apple tree beside the window.

"The top of that tree was grafted onto the strong apple base so that life would flow into it and produce good fruit. But there was a healthy branch which had to be cut off to make way for the graft. I am that branch."

Ernie struggled to keep up with Ben's explanation.

"People long ago found that they could get enormous power from breaking apart something smaller than a grain of sand. An atom should never be split, but when they managed to do this, it released a huge amount of power which could be used for evil or for good. I, too, am small, but when I am cut off, there will be life for a whole forest. Remember this!"

Ernest did mull this over, but could make no sense of it until much later.

***

The spring waters rose more than usual and refused to recede even after winter melt was complete. So there was serious discussion about when to begin a journey to safety, knowing that there would likely never be a return. To encourage people to commit to the venture, there was a ceremony of citizenship for the land beyond the bridge and people waited patiently in line for the tattoo of a four-tower bridge on their backs or their arms. Many people who had decided to move only to the immediate hilltop found the bridge tattoos attractive and paid a local artist to tattoo the same image on their own arms. These people laughed at talk of a real bridge.

The Pederson family hosted a rally where Ben addressed a crowd of newly convinced.

"My friends," he began, "do not be fooled by those who say there is no bridge, or that the journey is unnecessary. The Creator calls us and we know in our hearts which way to go."

"No, we don't!" shouted back someone in the crowd of newcomers. "All we have is your word for it. Apart from heading for higher land, what specific direction should we take?"

Ben chuckled, a deep warm chuckle, apparently amused by something which escaped his audience. "You are partially right, friend, in talking about heading for the hill country. That is the beginning. Trust me and you will find your way even in difficult terrain. But believe me when I tell you that even the hills will sink in the end."

"And then what will you recommend?" asked a woman scornfully.

"You will discover there is a bridge to safety."

"How could any bridge be the solution?" called back the woman. "Where would it take us? It's foolishness to talk about a bridge. A bridge to where? There is no land even close to this island. Our best bet is to get to the hills."

"The hills will certainly go down," replied Ben calmly. "But there is a bridge and I can show you the way to it. You have already seen and heard the way. If you set out and listen for my voice, you will not need a map." He chuckled again, then immediately grew serious.

"I myself am the map and you will discover that I am also the Bridge."

"He's crazy! He speaks in riddles!" cried out a voice in the crowd, then there were loud arguments and people began pushing and hitting each other.

"There is no point arguing!" shouted Ben above the din. "If you think I'm crazy, go back to your houses. Those who believe what I am saying, there is a day and a time to be ready at the northern exit to Newton. Your journey will begin in less than two weeks. You know the day."

With that he stepped down from the porch he had been standing on and strode away from the Pederson yard. Gradually the din subsided, people still muttering about his words, some declaring their renewed determination to stay with the Newton Council and work with what they knew, others agreeing among themselves that a journey of some sort was unavoidable, and they might as well leave, as Ben had suggested, within the next weeks. Perhaps, some suggested, Ben was referring to the fourth day of the fourth month, which was coming up soon—not a bad idea if one wanted the Creator's blessing. So those who committed to the journey began to plan for it and the departure time was arranged.

After the decision was made, excitement grew and more families joined. Ben continued daily to talk to people in distress over the loss of their houses, urging them to join those preparing to leave. Council was furious. Serena Knox proposed a way to stem the tide.

"Basically, there's one man who needs to disappear," she told a special meeting of Town Council. "He's telling everyone we're all going to sink. Well, maybe he should be the first to sink, then the rest of us can live in peace!" She looked meaningfully at each face around the table.

The next morning the body of Ben McAdams was found floating face down by Founders' Row. His body was pulled out by members of the Salvage crew who came across him and who were shocked at the death of the man they had worked with for years.

All day villagers came to see whether it could be true, that the leader of the journey was dead, then those who had been planning to leave Newton went away confused and downhearted. Council gave him a quiet burial.

Surprisingly, young Ernie Pederson took up the mantle. He called people together at his parents' home, and addressed the crowd boldly.

"Today, with the discovery of Ben's death, it seems that what he told us will not be possible without his leadership, that we will have to give up the journey. But realize this—somehow Ben knew we would be leaving without him. Remember that he said, '***Your*** journey will begin in less than two weeks.' Do we believe that he knew what he was talking about? I still believe that, and I will be there, ready, with my family, at the north exit to Newton just as we have planned. I hope to see you there, too!"

He spoke with such conviction and assurance that many in the crowd applauded. Judith could hardly believe that this was her younger brother speaking. People looked at each other with renewed hope and began again to talk about the departure.

And so it was that, instead of squashing the decision to leave, Ben's death actually made people more determined than ever.

Many now were keen to learn more of Ben's counsel for the journey. Fred Baker remembered that Ben had once declared, "Unless you walk in these shoes, you will never cross that bridge." Fred maintained that there was something very special about Ben's shoes, but the shoes had been buried with his body. All shoes in Tulemun were handmade by four leather workers, and Ben's had been made by Cy Albrecht. Cy found suddenly, in the month before the departure, that he had numerous orders for the same style of shoes as those he had made for Ben. Some people bought the shoes with no intention of going on thc journey; they were convinced that owning and wearing the shoes connected them with Ben and made them "people of the bridge", a bridge of the mind, they said, the only bridge which really mattered.

Someone (no one would admit it) actually tried to get the original shoes by digging up Ben's body. Dirt was piled on all sides of the hole where Ben's body had been buried but whoever did this left nothing, not even Ben's body, at the site. It was terribly upsetting, but the trip had to continue without any resolution to the robbery.

On the fourth day of the fourth month, that is, April 4th, they set out on a trek toward the eastern range of mountains. From the coast they started their journey, a motley crew of 143, most in young family groups with children, but there were a few grandparents and a few single adults, too. Many were neighbours or close friends. As Ernie had said, his family was all there—his parents Simon and Anne with his sister Judith, along with Uncle Vic, Aunt Jo, Harriet and Peter. Sammy Schmidt's older brother Henry came with his eight children, Hildy among them. Ernest was glad of that. With the group came two families who were convinced that any move away from coastal dampness was a healthy choice. Another couple, unconvinced of the bridge, still came along since their grandparents had originated in the eastern hill country; for them it was a desire to return to the old homestead, to find and relive the pioneer past.

Mr. Allister and the elderly couple from the hostel, Aida and Mikey, came to the road leading north in order to watch the departure. All three wished they could go, but knew the expedition would be impossibly hard for them. Aida sobbed and Mr. Allister, too, had tears in his eyes as they said their goodbyes to those setting out. Fred Baker, too, came and waved goodbye. Uncertain about leaving the business he had built, he chose in the end to remain. As he told Ernie, "It is the only responsible thing to do."

For most of the travelers there was a sense of being homeward bound, yet more—a quest, a pilgrimage toward a home they would recognize when they arrived even though (and here is the odd thing)—even though they had never actually seen it before!

Of course they had a map from the days of vehicles. Even if a supply of gas had been discovered, the cars were inoperable at this stage, rusted beyond repair, and the roads so broken by the Great Retaliation that driving more than a mile or two would have been impossible. So those leaving on the trek were reduced to walking, carrying belongings in wheelbarrows, overlaying these with planks to span the frequent chasms.

The plan was to walk about 6 hours a day, which Simon Pederson said would mean daily progress of about 15 miles, unless they were slowed down by too many chasms, rainy weather or sickness. Looking back later, it seemed there was always somebody sick or just dragging along, but the group pressed on together, carrying the youngest children when they complained.

It was fun at first, teenagers vying for who could outdo the others in giving piggyback rides to the little ones. Setting up tarps in late afternoon and preparing the campfire circles—these were chores eighteen year old Ernest enjoyed, particularly because he got to work with Hildy Schmidt, a girl not much younger than he. She had long curly blond hair, blue eyes, and a wonderful laugh. Away from the coast it was not hard to find dry wood, leaves and brush for kindling, and lodge pole pine branches strewn on the forest floor. The rich smell of pine needles baking in the sun was intoxicating. On sunny days they used magnifying glasses to start the flame, and on cloudy days fires could usually be started with a bow and drill, someone carefully shielding the little pile of leaves and twigs from wind and rain. Hildy became adept with the bow and Ernie felt exhilaration in being close to her while he shielded the fire starter. Also, he appreciated Hildy's questions about Ben, which allowed the young man to ramble comfortably in recollections of his mentor.

Their road to the mountains roughly paralleled the Baca River, which the group counted on for a supply of fresh water. They knew from the map where the road diverged from the Baca to loop around a canyon before rejoining the water, so on those days when there would be no available water, water jugs were filled up and that weight was added to the wheelbarrows.

Food was another matter. People had loaded up with sea salt, honey, and flour before leaving. These were measured out sparingly each day of travel. For meat they relied on two rifles which provided dinners of quail, grouse, hare and mule deer. Eventually the ammunition ran out and Uncle Victor came to the rescue with his knowledge of how to manufacture gunpowder. It had been around for 900 years, he said, and there was no reason they couldn't make some themselves, if the group could set aside a couple of days from travel plans.

He pointed out that only three ingredients were needed, of which two could definitely be found and the third was a possibility. Charcoal was the easiest to obtain, particularly good from burning dead branches of Cottonwood and Willow growing along the Baca River. Sulfur was not much harder because they were in volcanic country where the yellowish deposit could occasionally be seen on gentle slopes of gravelly ground. The smell of rotten eggs was distinct. Hardest to find was saltpetre, potassium nitrate. Uncle Vic said he had an idea about that. Leaving base camp, he led a group of men and older teens up to a cave from which bats had flown out the previous evening. Bat dung, it turned out, is a natural source of saltpetre, and they found it in abundance in the recesses of the cave. Ernest's uncle supervised the collection of each item and carefully ground each one, when sun dried, with a mortar and pestle made from rounded river rocks. The formula was well known, he said, ever since the time of Mongols in Europe or before that, the Chinese: 75-15-10. Fortunately, the climate close to the mountains was dry, because the powder could be ruined by humidity. Uncle Vic told the others the two rifles used to this point were basically useless without standard ammunition, so they would rely now on the muzzleloader Ernie's Father had given him on his sixteenth birthday. That would take the powder, and they could even fire river pebbles with it. The young man felt quite proud when his uncle said this, since it was the one thing Ernie had chosen to bring on the trek, even though the powder had long ago been used up. To him it represented a coming of age, his father's acknowledgement of manhood. And now it would be used to provide for the journey! They all watched in fascination, the uncle talking enthusiastically as he rammed freshly mixed powder down the barrel.

There was a loud blast as powder shot out. Simultaneously the gun leaped from his grasp, catapulted into the air, then lay smoking a few feet away. Uncle Victor rolled on the ground clutching his right hand. No one wanted to repeat this experiment even if, as Victor insisted, it was a matter of measuring more carefully. By general consensus, the idea of mixing their own gunpowder ceased to be an option. The group would have to resort to more predictable methods of obtaining meat.

Since the Great Retaliation, when so many supplies had become scarce, many people made slings and had become fairly accurate with them. With a good sling and practice, it was possible to pick off ground birds and even an occasional hare. And there were little river trout in the Baca, hard to catch and small, but available for an hour of evening fishing.

Routines were established for rising with the sun, eating together, breaking camp, carrying assignments, stopping for regular breaks, setting up camp at dusk, supper duties and campfire circle. There were days of wind or rain when they just stayed in one place. But in general, travel was possible and the group of 143 pushed on.

Once through the first mountain pass, they came across an old homestead, long abandoned, and there the couple with ties to the Eastern hill country decided to settle. There was a creek and an overgrown orchard which they both felt excited about. Ernest's father and Uncle Victor urged them to continue the journey, but the couple had never thought the Bridge story credible, and was even less inclined to follow Victor's advice after the gunpowder fiasco. They pointed out that the old farm was on a high point of land compared to the valley to which all the rest were heading. The whole group camped on the old homestead for a couple of days, then there were tearful farewells and the couple was left to pioneer their new property.

From the old orchard a path descended beside the creek to a marshy lake shore, then beyond to open rolling plain country, dry with coarse grass tufts, sage brush, and the sound of crickets. This vast rolling plain was crisscrossed with deer trails and surrounded by distant hills or mountains. Without any map for this territory, the group agreed to aim for one particular saddle-backed mountain far to the east. They ignored trails which they came across unless these led in the general direction of the Saddle.

Day after monotonous day they wandered across the plain, occasionally resting by rock pools where rain water had collected. In one such rest area, they noticed rounded rocks strewn across the landscape. "Thunder eggs", Victor explained, then cracked one open to reveal amethyst crystals. Younger children ran around, excitedly cracking open rocks, showing their treasures to each other, then piling these into the wheelbarrows.

Ernie intervened. "The rocks are beautiful, but they are so heavy. We carry only what we have to, children." He persuaded them instead to make a pyramid of their treasures, a mound to mark the way for any other travelers. Hildy Schmidt looked on with admiration and Ernie, reddening, felt a pride of growing manhood.

The ground was sloping up now, harder going, but forming a gradual ascent toward the Saddle. There was no longer any brush, only wispy grass growing out of rock crevices. Water pools were also fewer and most had evaporated. This became the greatest concern after two or three days. Then, when the Saddle, shrouded by thick fog, seemed only half a kilometer away, they experienced their greatest tragedy: old Dr. Van Erden died. He had stumbled along valiantly until that point. His daughter Marika, a single woman in her fifties, had doubted his ability to make the trek, and now was bitterly regretting their participation. She looked accusingly at Ernie and his father Simon.

"We can't even give him a decent burial here—it's all rock!" There was silence as the leaders looked at each other, trying for some kind way to reply. Then Ernie spoke decisively, with more authority than his youth.

"Ben would say we give this fine man a good burial, even though it means going down below the tree line." There was an awkward lull in conversation, and Ernest's father was the voice of reason.

"Of course that is what we would all like to do, but we have to deal with the reality of having gained this altitude already, being so close to the Saddle that a descent would set us back days. Perhaps we could find enough rock to create a grave right here." Marika was sobbing. Ernie put his arm around her shoulder. For a moment he seemed unsure whether to break with his father's counsel, then he surprised himself by speaking so firmly.

"We will never be sorry for taking time for others. It was Ben's way and it must be ours also."

People sighed, looked deflated, but agreed to make a descent to the valley. This turned out to be easier than they had supposed. Among the trees close to a river bed, they found the soil easy digging. All 140 of them stood solemnly around the grave, spoke a blessing over Dr. Van Erden, thanking the Creator for his life, then filled in the hole and placed four stones at the corners. Four saplings were cut to angle in like a tent frame from the corner stones, binding them at head height where they met in the middle—a pointer to heaven. Marika quietly thanked each of the leaders. The group was exhausted, physically and emotionally, but felt relieved to have taken the day to honour Marika's father. They realized, too, as they settled down in the evening, that descent to the valley had led them to a fresh water supply, the first in several days.

In the morning light Ernie wandered along a deer trail to where he could see the mountain they had descended yesterday. The fog had lifted now and he was shocked to realize that the hill they had been climbing ended abruptly with a cliff! So there had been no gentle ascent to The Saddle after all—and they had actually come close to the cliff edge as they stumbled on in yesterday's fog! Thank God for the decision to come down when they did! Ernie lost no time in rushing back and bringing the leaders to see what he had just discovered. Rising gently from the valley floor close to where they stood was a well-trodden trail zigzagging up toward the Saddle. They stood, amazed at their good fortune. Ernie was jubilant.

"It's like Ben used to tell me—choose what is right, and you will find that God is in your detours."

***

Hours of slogging up the switch-back trail took them higher by far than the first mountain pass. Pausing for breath, they looked back at the way they had come, trying to identify the old homestead where the pioneering couple had remained. From here they noticed with amazement that the distant glint of sea water almost surrounded and cut off that first mountain! Simon observed solemnly that people really had to climb to gain perspective, and they continued their ascent in stunned silence.

Finally, the path began to level out, to widen and become a road. An enormous bridge tower loomed ahead. Excitement gripped the travelers and spurred them on another half kilometre to the very top of The Saddle from where they could see the road approaching this bridge. The whole group, bone-tired from the climb, stopped to survey the scene—and there was a collective gasp or groan of dismay.

From their vantage point they could now see below them, stretching out as far as the eye could see, a vast tent city along the shore closest to the bridge entrance. There were other survivors apart from the people of Tulemun—thousands of them! They scarcely had time to understand this before a greater revelation took their breath away.

The bridge access itself hovered inexplicably in the air hundreds of feet above. So they had made it all this way in vain! There was no way to access the bridge for any of these people! In disbelief, Ernie and his group made their way downhill to join the others, people sitting, eating or conversing with each other in languages Ernie did not recognize. A tall man came to meet them, smiling, and extending a hand of friendship to Ernie. His style of clothing and his accent were nothing like those from Tulemun.

"We have been waiting for you, dear friends. We know that no one goes on the bridge until the last people arrive." He motioned for the newcomers to sit down close to the tents, then beckoned to Ernie to follow him back to the hilltop. Sighing and confused, Ernest accompanied the man, stumbling back up the hill to where they could see far back along the way they had come. "Now it will happen," said his new friend eagerly, shielding his eyes and peering back along the road. "Watch!"

As they stood waiting, Ernie simply had to ask. "Did you and your people also perhaps know Ben McAdams? He was—he is—so important." At mention of Ben's name, the tall man beside him showed no sign of recognition, but listened as Ernie described the town planner who had mentored him and encouraged their group to prepare for the journey. Ernest told of Ben's strange wisdom, his kindness and his uncanny certainty about the way the Creator would guide them to the Bridge. As he told about Ben's death and their subsequent adventures, the other man became intensely interested.

"No," he said wistfully, "I never met Ben. It seems there may be things you know that I have only guessed."

A tiny black cloud had formed close to the mountain pass which they had negotiated a few days ago. Movement in the sky could be detected even at that great distance; evidently a thunder storm was sweeping over the pass. Ernest noted an ominous anvil shape forming, then a breeze stirred grass at his own feet. A sound like an approaching train rose from the direction of the pass. It was a continuous rumble and the sky over the closest valley was rapidly darkening with an eerie greenish yellow in the black. A ghostly funnel-shaped cloud extended, snaked down from the black anvil all the way to the ground, oscillating hypnotically like the body of a cobra. Gathering over their own hill now, dark cumulus cloud swirled, boiled and billowed high. The grass at their feet suddenly was motionless. Something fell beside Ernest and he was shocked to see hail the size of a chestnut. Then the storm unleashed and hundreds of white chestnuts along with heavy rain pelted them as they ran for the group downhill.

Branches and whole trees were falling behind them on the very path they had come down! The roar now was intense and the wind impossible to lean against. People huddled together, caught between unbelievable wind and the sea. Tent pegs yanked from the ground and canvases, tent poles, tables ripped up into the air. People were on their knees now, crying, clinging to each other and praying aloud. Then, suddenly, they were in the centre of the funnel itself and felt themselves swept off their feet, lifted up, some still holding hands, limp rag dolls drawn up in the vortex—and they knew it was the end.

Remarkably, the wind seemed promptly to abate and they found that their feet had been set down upon the bridge! Like waking from a nightmare, there was no sound or sign of the storm they had come through. High overhead there were patches of blue in the mist beyond the bridge upon which they stood.

It was unlike any bridge they had ever seen before, made of an unusual metal, suspended by cables which disappeared into mist far above. The deck itself climbed very gradually until it also disappeared into mist, so there was no way of knowing whether it would ever begin to descend somewhere else. Of course, it must.

Ernie noticed a young woman strangely dressed who had also descended from the column of wind. She had a child she sheltered in a pack in front of her and held the hand of an old man who leaned against her, exhausted.

"Do you know what this Bridge is made of?" Ernie asked her.

"Is it a bridge?" she said haltingly in English. "I was not sure. No, I don't know what it is made of, but I knew it would be here. God provides."

"Yes, absolutely," replied Ernie. He had a sense of being close to a familiar friend. "There is much about this Bridge I do not understand. But I know it will not collapse. It will bear the weight of us all."

And, he thought to himself with a smile, it already has. The man walking ahead looked very like Dr. Van Erden, whom they had buried just yesterday. Beside him hobbled three older people who seemed familiar. Aida, Mikey and Mr. Allister! But how could that be, since they had been too weak to attempt the journey? Perhaps, in their hearts…

Ernie's reverie was interrupted by an awful thought. How terribly sad that Ben could not be here, too! Ben, who had encouraged them all to set out, who had worked so hard to make this happen. Ben, whose very death seemed to propel them on the journey. Ben, whose way of dealing with things had guided them in choices along the way. He had indeed been the map. In fact, if it weren't for Ben, Ernie thought, they wouldn't be here at all.

Above him he heard a deep chuckle, a chuckle he recognized immediately. When he looked up, only cables were visible. The chuckle sounded again—unmistakable, but ahead this time. Incredulous, bursting with joy, Ernie began to run forward.

CPSIA information can be obtained
at www.ICGtesting.com
Printed in the USA
BVHW081127111221
623748BV00004B/21